W9-AQA-733

ABOUT THE AUTHOR

Jim Pierce is an insurance executive living in Houston, Texas. His ties to the Presidency start with a distant connection to Franklin Pierce, the 14th President of the United States. More recently, his uncle George H. W. Bush served as the 41st President, and his first cousin George W. Bush was the 43rd American to reside in the White House as Commander-in-Chief. While spending his career in the insurance business, Jim's love of history began early and has never waned. His reverence for the acts of the Founding Fathers in the 18th century through to the words and deeds of Abraham Lincoln remains steadfast. Jim is married and has four children. He and his wife Dabney are enjoying their first grandchild, whose first name, as luck would have it, is Pierce.

Copyright © 2022 Jim Pierce
All rights reserved. This book or any portion thereof may not
be reproduced or used in any manner whatsoever without the
express written permission of the publisher except for the use
of brief quotations in a book review.

Cover Art © Lauren Leihgeber
All rights reserved. Used with permission.

Paperback ISBN: 9798986480596
eBook ISBN: 9798986480589
Hardcover ISBN: 9798986480572

First Edition: June 2022

Published by Auto Book Bots
New York, NY 10003

DEDICATION

This book is dedicated to Professor Roy T. Wortman of Kenyon College. Now deceased, Professor Wortman made history come alive for his students. His name will live through the Roy T. Wortman Chair in History at Kenyon.

AUTHOR'S NOTE

So much has been written about Abe Lincoln and the Civil War years but not every holograph can make you appreciate your present. Therefore, I sat down to write a story, completely fabricated yet steeped in history. Of particular note is that I have assigned mischievous roles to two of President Lincoln's generals. I have taken liberties, and that is what one does when writing fiction; even historical fiction. The entire premise of this story revolves around something that went horribly wrong for the Union's pursuit of victory in the first year and a half of the conflagration. I have taken these liberties to provide a possible explanation as to why utter incompetence became symbolic of the Union's attempts to prosecute a successful war strategy.

I have tried diligently to accurately and chronologically depict many events of that time and create viable images of the characters described throughout these pages. While some of the names herein are very real, it does not mean they did everything suggested in the narrative. At the risk of overkill, it is very important that you, the reader, are cognizant of these nuances. The timeline for the battles and the details enumerated herein are all written to be accurate. If there is a mistake, it is an honest one. The vast majority of the characters mentioned in this book are real. They existed in the roles described in the following pages. Some characters are entirely fictitious. Neither they nor their alleged actions actually happened. If you are dying to separate fact from fiction while you read, the

Epilogue will help you to do so. On the other hand, if you choose to get lost in the story and come back to earth after finishing the book, the Epilogue will be waiting for you.

I hope you will be entertained by what you are about to read. When you are finished with it, I also fervently wish for you to understand more about the impossible job Lincoln somehow managed to make possible. He was an amazing man, and no small part of what he accomplished is why we can enjoy the freedoms that so many Americans have come to take for granted. Preserving the Union meant everything to him. He never lost his focus on that singular goal. If you make your only goal to not put this book down until you are finished, I don't think you will regret it!

CONTENTS

WITH GRATITUDE

This book may not have happened but for the review of the first several pages by Jean Becker, former Chief of Staff to President George H. W. Bush. Jean perused the truncated draft because, and in her words,

"First reaction: I couldn't put it down. I was sad when I got to the end."

That was all I needed to carry on. She then helped by reading and commenting on the balance of the draft. I also relied upon my daughter Clemmie Pierce Martin to provide a fresh (and younger) set of eyes on the narrative. She attended Plan II at the University of Texas, and for those of you who don't know, that means she can write.

Lastly, I would like to thank Bob Rose, haberdasher to the stars (and regular folk such as yours truly) in downtown Houston, Texas. Bob is a voracious reader. I sought his opinion about the story itself, and as a bonus, he found myriad typos. Thank you, Bob.

"When Sorrows Come, They Come Not Single Spies, but in Battalions."

William Shakespeare

Hamlet (Act IV - Scene IV)

THE MAP

Maryland

3.

Potomac

5.
4.

2.

7.

Virginia

6.

0   10   20   30   mi

1. White House
2. Richmond
3. President's Cottage
   at soldiers home
4. Battle of Manassas
5. Arlington
6. Shenandoa Valley
7. Peninsula Campaign

PROLOGUE

Abe Lincoln traveled undercover to Washington D.C. (at that time, there was no District of Columbia) to be sworn in as the 16th President of the United States. Situations were already that terrible. The rail-splitter from Illinois was hardly the odds-on favorite to be the Republican nominee and was even less favored to win the election.

His victory was anything but the permanent (or, for that matter, palliative) cure a dangerously divided nation needed. He was seen by mainstream Republicans as a gangly commoner from the Midwest and by the southern Democrats as an extreme threat to their way of life and that "peculiar institution" some referred to as slavery.

Even his discreet trip to Washington didn't happen without drama. A group of southerners who had taken extreme umbrage at the notion of his presidency tried to eliminate him before he could even put his hand on the bible. Obviously, they did not succeed. It fell to John Wilkes Booth just four years later to commit that horrible act.

This book does not focus on the attempts (unsuccessful or otherwise) to murder Abe Lincoln. It is no secret that President Lincoln became extremely frustrated at the pace with which the succession of generals prosecuted the war against the south. This story addresses his first year and a half as President, the confluence of events, and people conspiring to give the Confederate states time to prepare for war.

CHAPTER ONE
SEEDS OF DECEIT

The White House,
March 21, 1861

Abe Lincoln was the most misunderstood man. He always had been, but while it didn't matter much before, it did now that he was President of the United States.

"I can only imagine the anguish ahead of us, Mary. My God, you know, it will be a bit like stringing a pig up by its hind feet long enough for its blood to start dripping out of its eyes and ears... God, the squealing is terrible... I have no choice but to hang this pig." Abe Lincoln looked out of his bedroom window at the White House lawn leading into the swampy marshlands, which stretched nearly as far as he could see. A few roads meandered vertically and horizontally through the largely undeveloped land. He had just been the President for around three weeks. Mary was there with him, quietly darning little Willie's socks. She hadn't heard a word he had spoken.

Candles and some gas lights illuminated the White House incessantly, but it seemed as if no amount of light helped the President sift through the muddled issues confronting him. A growing southern army presence was milling menacingly outside the city. Fort Sumter stood perilously close to abdicating the gray-clad troops pressuring its walls. An uneasy air permeated the core of the nation's political heart. "Same old, same old, Mary... it will be might which determines right, and precious little else," he sighed.

"Oh, Abe, what are you going on about?" quipped Mary Todd Lincoln. She sat perched on a new overstuffed-down chair designed with pallid color overwhelmed by an English fabric full of colorful greens and blues. Their youngest son's socks lay strewn on the floor around her feet. Willie Lincoln had an uncommon way about him; a model son in almost all respects, he nonetheless chewed holes in his socks for no apparent reason. This odd trait kept his mother busy trying to keep his undersized feet warm.

"What are you saying about pigs anyway, Abe? What does hanging a pig have to do with whether it's light out or night?" Mary replayed what she thought she had heard over the past few minutes and posed her question as logically as one who hadn't been paying any attention at all.

"Never mind, Mary," the President replied. "I suppose it's my problem. Yes, the time is nigh upon us when I must decide how to eradicate this growing threat to our fledgling nation." Lincoln buried his eyes in his palms and pressed hard, so the colors flashed brilliantly in the black holes beyond which he so desperately wished to see. Looking out again across the acres of green, he said, "No guns, a rag-tag army, no real support from the people, and the fearsome will of a rapidly developing enemy army poised to initiate action against us... I know I can overcome all of this, Mary. I wonder if the sycophants I put in my Cabinet can put aside their petty politics and serve their nation in its time of need."

"Abe, did you know that we can eat whatever we'd like to here at the White House? You just need to ask Samuel, our porter. He's seen five Presidents come and go. He's a lovely man. He'll take care of you." Marry said, not paying the least attention to her husband's apprehensions

"If he's so eager for me to eat, I'd better get a food taster," Lincoln mumbled.

The White House, March 28, 1861

The prospect of war weighed heavily on the minds of all men. On none did it weigh more heavily than Lincoln's. A few days before he died in 1865, he told his son Robert that each heavy line on his weary-looking face represented a major battle. On this morning, however, as he prepared to convene a Cabinet meeting, the crags had just begun

3

to form. It would not be long before those lines looked like hedgerows.

The Cabinet met in a room nearby the family living quarters on the second floor of the White House. (Latter day Americans have correctly come to think of the West Wing as the place where the majority of White House business is conducted. That notwithstanding, the West Wing wasn't actually constructed until 1902, during Teddy Roosevelt's time in office.) It was in the family living quarters area that most of the strategies to choke the life out of the secessionist movement were developed. He had one or perhaps two men on his Cabinet he could call friends. Looking across the table at his Secretary of War, Simon Cameron, Lincoln knew that he wasn't one of them. No President had ever entered office with more people and factions aligned against him. He was an outsider, seemingly something of a bumbler. His penetrating eyes made people nervous. Initially, his Cabinet choices were ridiculed as the act of a naive President trying to placate potential enemies. Most people thought it was a tremendous error to staff his Cabinet with various personalities who, one way or another, wished to sit in his chair.

Abe Lincoln had no intention of mollifying his detractors. He believed the enemy known was better than the one not known, and by God, he was going to keep the enemy close at hand. As he prepared to address the agenda for the day, he looked around the room and thought to himself, "Good Lord, I really do need to have a food taster on staff."

Clearing his throat, he said, "Gentlemen, I believe Thomas Paine coined the phrase, *'These are the times which try men's souls.'* Well, indeed, they are. For the past six weeks, I have sought your counsel and input. I have worked closely with General Scott, and preparations are clearly underway for the most massive assault on the nation that our young country has yet experienced. You may recall my inaugural address when I pontificated to our southern brothers. *'In your hands, my dissatisfied fellow countrymen, is the momentous issue of civil war. We can have no conflict without you yourselves being aggressors.'* Well, they came, they listened, and they left. Now they prepare for war... now they taunt us at Fort Sumter, and soon their forces will gather within miles of this city."

He continued after a brief pause, "Gentlemen, we must preserve our United States. To not do so is to allow the noblest experiment in human history to needlessly falter. We are not perfect. We do not cast stones lest our own windows be broken. I am reminded of Thomas Jefferson, who, when surveying the inequities in our burgeoning nation, uttered the words, *'I tremble for my country when I think that God is just.'* How prophetic was this man? Doesn't Jefferson Davis pray to the same God as I? Do we not have brothers, cousins, and uncles against whom we are about to engage in unparalleled carnage? God is just and that, gentlemen, is one reason we will prevail. Another reason we will prevail is that we have the physical might to win. Now... six weeks ago, I asked several of you for reports on our industrial, food, supply, and medical bases. To date, I've received nothing of substance from any of you. I also asked you for recommendations regarding Fort Sumter. Shall we abandon the fort or hold our ground? You have given me answers, but I sense no consensus or conviction. Let me be perfectly succinct in expressing my feelings. You may not like me. That is of no consequence, but you have accepted positions in my Cabinet during a time of your country's dire need."

Lincoln paused and then bored into the group with his last salvo, "You will work with me, or you will resign from your positions. Is that clear?" The silence was deafening, but Lincoln noted affirmative nods from every attendee.

"Good," he said. "I will ask General Scott to arrange for Fort Sumter to be re-supplied. This action will not provoke the secessionists. They will have to take it upon themselves for the first step. My firm belief is that they will do so. As cold-hearted as it may seem, my thoughts are now past Fort Sumter. War is nigh, Gentlemen, and plans must be made now. Just so we all are aligned, I want to march into Virginia by July. Firm and decisive action can end this insurrection before the

New Year. I will need your help. I trust I'll have it."

Pausing for a few seconds, Lincoln rose from the table, thanked them for coming, and disappeared into the second-floor living quarters.

John Nicolay slipped into Lincoln's living room about an hour after the Cabinet members had disbanded. The President sat in one of Mary's overstuffed chairs. He had turned it around to face one of the windows looking out over the south lawn. His feet were up on the windowsill, and he appeared to be in a deep, brooding trance.

Nicolay was the President's, right-hand man. He ran Lincoln's schedule and looked after various personal affairs. In a short period of time, he had made himself rather indispensable. He was, for all intents and purposes, Lincoln's Chief of Staff (this title, however, would only come into existence during the Eisenhower administration ninety years later). Lincoln stirred the third time after Nicolay said, "Sir." He slowly turned his head to the left to gaze upon his young attendant. "Mr. Nicolay, I thank you for giving me an hour's escape. I needed it, although I dare say I do not feel much better for it. Well, boy, what did those men say after I left them wiggling like worms on their chairs."

Nicolay smiled and went on to say, "Mr. President, if you do not mind me saying, I don't think you'll be winning any popularity contests with your Cabinet... but, then again, you aren't really trying to, are you?" Laughing again, he continued. "I think I could have heard a pin drop for at least a minute. Nobody would have said anything. And you're right; there was some incredible squirming taking place. I believe it was Secretary Seward who broke the ice."

"How did he do so?" the President inquired.

"He said, 'God damn it to hell, how do you like them apples?' and then he just got up and left."

"Then, what happened?"

"Then the rest of them, Cameron, Smith, Bates, Blair, Welles, and Chase just followed him out of the door and downstairs. No one said

6

a thing."

"I don't remember saying anything about apples, John," the President said.

"Apples, sir? Oh, apples... well, I think that's just an expression; a colloquialism of sorts."

"Is it now, Mr. Nicolay? I do thank you for helping me remedy my inept grasp of the subtleties in our language."

"Ah, sorry, Sir," Nicolay stammered.

Nicole took his leave while Lincoln looked out of the window in time to see Mary disembarking the carriage. In her wake were two attendants loaded down with fabrics destined to adorn the White House windows. "Good Lord," he muttered as he sat back again to stare out into Washington's abyss.

Washington, D.C., April 18, 1861

Three hundred pounds of lard sat in a corner booth in Callaghan's Grillroom, a half-mile down Pennsylvania Avenue from the White House. General Winfield Scott had served his country with honor and distinction. He was a decorated war hero. He was also on his last legs and wholly unacquainted with the methodologies of warfare in the 1860s. The President knew he would have to replace General Scott but what he didn't know was with whom. General McDowell was Scott's chosen successor. In Lincoln's eyes, McDowell seemed more of a prig than a leader of men. The President was trying hard to give him the benefit of his doubt.

An officious young man of slender build and a paper-thin mustache glided inside the door, spotted General Scott, and immediately moved in his direction. The General was just finishing a pint of beer when he heard, "General Scott, sir, if I might have a few minutes of your time, sir." The voice was unmistakably that of a southern aristocrat.

"Sit down, boy," said the general, whose attention had shifted

7

effortlessly to the lamb chops monopolizing his plate. "What do you have for me?"

The man leaned over the table within twelve inches of General Scott's corpuscular face.

"Jesus! Son, Sit back, for Christ's sake. You'll spit all over my chops," bellowed the General.

"Sorry, sir," said the young man, immediately moving back and then uttering in a hushed tone, "President Davis sends his regards."

"And I send mine to him."

"General Scott, President Davis needs time. He needs to know that the Union army will not be prepared to move effectively for at least six months."

Scott looked at the messenger for what seemed like an eternity. All the while, he chewed on his chop. Contorting his face in seeming frustration, he lifted his bloated hand and removed a worked-over piece of gristle from his mouth. "You tell President Davis he'll have his reprieve. You tell him that I said so. He needs to leave the tactics to me, but he'll have the time he needs to build his army. Tell him I don't think we'll ever be ready. But, in any event, we will not move for at least three months. Now go away, boy."

The messenger took his cue and left as unobtrusively as he had arrived. General Scott looked ponderous, but what was distracting him soon dissipated when a plate of fried eggs and bacon replaced the lamb chop bones.

Across town Simon Cameron stood in his parlor, pouring two Armagnacs; one for himself and another for the dashing General George McClellan.

"You are a student of war, are you not, General?

"I am, indeed, the best West Point has ever produced, if you'll pardon my modesty," he replied.

"And can this war be won?"

"Mr. Secretary," the rigid-backed McClellan responded, "this won't ever be a war. This skirmish will be finished by Christmas. Their commanders are well-regarded, sir, but they are old. Their tactics would have worked brilliantly in the War of 1812. Their troops lack funds. Without funding, there are no supplies without supplies, no morale... no morale, no troops. It's a circle of self-destruction. I will... I mean, of course, *we* will route them."

"You have, of course, been sharing your ideas with General Scott?" The Secretary inquired.

McClellan looked at the Secretary of War, sipped his Armagnac, and replied, "No, sir... in my humble opinion that would be a complete waste of time. If Lee and the others are ready to conquer the British of 1812, our good General Scott's tactics date clear back to 1776. Good heavens, with all due respect, of course, the man is a dinosaur. He cannot lead the Union army on to Pennsylvania Avenue, much less into Virginia."

"Who can lead our army then, General?"

McClellan locked his eyes onto Cameron's, and then with a majestic bow, said, "At your service, sir."

"Why am I not surprised by your response, General?" he chuckled while raising his glass in a silent toast to his drinking companion.

Later that evening, as Cameron prepared for bed, he mused over his discussion with the young General. Pouring water into his washbasin, he splashed some on his clammy face (Cameron was perpetually moist. He always kept a wash towel ready to wipe away the cumulative effects of the day). Tonight was certainly no exception, particularly after five Armagnacs with the General. Cameron looked smugly into the mirror. "Our next great General is mine. I will run him, and I will ride his victory over the secessionist states right to the White House in 1864. The bumpkin will be a distant memory. I will bring dignity to the White House. I will..." his voice trailed off as he realized (albeit belatedly) that he was working himself into an outright speech. This

9

would have been fine, but for the fact that the audience he was whipping into a frenzy was his reflection. Perhaps even more absurd was the fact that the President's opponent in the 1864 election would ultimately be the General who had just left his house.

Richmond, Virginia, April 19, 1861

Much had transpired in the past week. Fort Sumter had fallen to South. Virginia would soon vote, overwhelmingly, to join the Confederacy, and Robert E. Lee had chosen his allegiance, and he would fight for his home state.

Henry Memminger was admitted into Jefferson Davis' office at 9:30 a.m. The President of the Confederate States of America huddled over the circular mahogany table, accompanied by Generals; Joseph E. Johnston, Robert E. Lee, and two men that Memminger did not recognize. Davis had appointed Johnston as Commander of the Army of Northern Virginia and Lee as one of the five full generals representing the South, but with specific control of forces in Virginia. It was as clear to Davis as it was to Lincoln that Virginia would be the venue to test both armies first. Davis had chosen a stately private residence in Richmond as his presidential headquarters. A workmanlike atmosphere permeated the entire house. The war was in its nascent stage, yet a somber aura already prevailed across the country. The enormity of the challenge faced by the southern states escaped no one.

Davis looked up as the newcomer entered the room.

"Ah, Henry, it's good to see you, boy. Another successful trip into the heart and soul of the enemy, I hope."

"Yes, sir... I saw my acquaintance last night. He has taken your request on board. He wanted me to tell you to leave the tactics to him and to expect no Union troop movement before July."

General Lee was visibly relieved. "That at least gives us some time to develop supply lines and train our army. Not enough time, mind you, but time."

It was interesting that President Davis asked Robert E. Lee this question, bypassing his senior General Johnston. It was almost as though Davis had a vision that Joseph Johnston would be wounded and taken out of action a year later. It seemed as though he knew Bob Lee was the man upon whom the southern cause would come to rely.

"Have you considered a preemptive strike at the capital, General?" asked Davis.

"I have, but no matter how much disarray the Union army is purported to be in, I do not believe a foray into their home turf, as it were, would result in anything but an unmitigated disaster for our cause."

"You are the tactician, General," replied Jefferson Davis, "and I defer to your judgment. And of course, to you too, General Johnston. Just remember that we cannot win a war of attrition. They have more men, money, and industry. But do you know what we have? We have a cause. And that cause has every red-blooded American southerner ready to sacrifice everything to see it through to its fruition. Just so we are all very clear, the cause to which I make reference is not slavery! The status of the negroes is what it is. Sure, we can get our landed gentry riled up over being told what they can do and can't do, but this cause, gentlemen, is our southern cause! This is about getting out from under the yoke of northern control, once and for all. No one will be beholden to them. We will control our destiny, our trade, our agriculture, our industry. We must take matters into our hands. Now is the time! We mustn't let this opportunity slip through fate's fingers."

He turned back to the young messenger and spoke, "Henry, you studied at Harvard with Lincoln's assistant, John Nicolay. Did you

11

not?"

"Yes, sir... in fact, we were fast friends in school."

"And is Mr. Nicolay susceptible in any way to the powers of persuasion?"

"Nicolay is a fine man, as far as I know, Mr. President. I am told he is loyal to Abe Lincoln, and only Abe Lincoln."

"Does he know of your loyalties in this transgression?"

"I haven't seen him for two years, and when we last crossed paths, I was working for my father's bank. I dare say he will suspect me for what I am...a Richmond man through and through."

"Ah, yes, the bank... oh, by the way, Henry, your father will be my Secretary of the Treasury. I've asked him to develop a Confederate currency and figure out a way to make it worth something."

Henry grinned, "My father has always liked challenges."

"Well," chuckled Davis, "he has one now, doesn't he? Anyway, Henry, I need to know what Lincoln is going to do with our General Scott. Is our good friend General McDowell going to assume responsibility for the Union army? If so, when? I don't suppose Mr. Nicolay could unwittingly fill some blanks in for us?"

"I can only run it up the flagpole and see if it flies, sir," Memminger responded.

"Then do so, and let me know the results soonest. Keep up the good work, Henry."

Henry took his President's words of encouragement as his cue, and nodding to the three men; he headed for the door. The group he left behind was once again hunched over the table before he left the room. As he closed the door behind him, he recognized his

President's voice saying, "And what are your thoughts, General McDowell?"

"Well, Mr. President, there is no doubt that I should be given the command. Scott is not at all well. Tell me, sir," McDowell shifted ground, "about that Memminger boy, who is his contact in Washington?"

"Please do not get offended when I tell you it is best you do not know," President Davis responded succinctly and moved on.

Jefferson Davis had more than one card up his sleeve. He had Generals Scott and McDowell in his pocket. Neither knew of the other's traitorous activity. Both were in positions to wreak havoc on Lincoln's early war plans. Each, in his own way, intended to do just that.

"Incredible," Henry thought to himself as he descended to the first floor of the house.

"Irvin McDowell is a general in the Union army and will most likely lead them into battle against us. I wonder if Lincoln has anyone on his side."

Being the son of prominent South Carolina banker Christopher Memminger, Henry was cut from the same cloth as his father. He was an excellent sportsman in school, Phi Beta Kappa at Harvard, and acknowledged as a "quick study" in his infant banking career. He had jumped at the opportunity to be at the service of Jefferson Davis. He quickly proved his mettle by networking in Washington and developing his information gold mine in the person of Winfield Scott. Who would have thought the venerable general would harbor so strong an abiding respect for southern traditions that he would betray the Union? No one, of course, and that was why Henry's contact was invaluable.

Traveling from Richmond to Washington, D.C. in ordinary times was

13

not a particularly daunting task. However, these were not ordinary times. Henry found himself successful at convincing southern pickets that he was one of them. While a few miles down the road, he slipped into his most affected New England accent acquired during his Harvard tenure. He traveled in Union territory as a banker, still conducting business affairs in Confederate territory. This was not entirely uncommon. Most businessmen spent hours figuring out ways to maintain links with their southern or northern clients. The pursuit of profit has long provided mankind with tremendous powers of rationalization. It would not be until July of that year that Lincoln forbade any commerce between northern and southern businesses.

Henry decided not to stay the night in Richmond. Part of him wanted very much to see Janie Frank. Two years his junior, Janie was the daughter of his parents' best friends. She and Henry had grown up together. He was gallant and adventuresome; she was ravishingly beautiful and smart as a whip. While they knew each other like brother and sister, there was also a physical attraction, which had never been explored. Both of them knew their physical and spiritual union was inevitable, yet events had conspired to prevent their union. For as long as he could remember, one thing above all which separated Janie from any woman he would ever meet was her scent. He remembered her smell from times when they would hide in hollowed-out logs together. Maybe they were four or perhaps five years old, he couldn't recall. It didn't matter. He could close his eyes any time, at any place, and smell Janie Frank. The thought of burying his nose in her neck was enough to distract him. She was his olfactory heaven on earth. Alas, Janie would have to wait. The affairs of the state were pressing, and Henry Memminger was helping shape history.

He reached Washington D.C. by nightfall and immediately proceeded to the Willard Hotel. Henry did not think that his character lent itself to cloak and dagger charades. Whenever in Union territory, he was Henry Memminger, the banker. In the morning, he would become

14

reacquainted with his old friend John Nicolay.

Abe Lincoln lay in bed pondering over the events of the past week. Since he last convened his Cabinet nearly a week before, he had seen neither hide nor hair of them. Washington was not a big town. These men were avoiding him, and he knew it.

"Does it have to stay white?" His thoughts were interrupted by Mary's question.

"Does what have to stay white, Mary?"

"The White House, of course, Abraham."

"What do you have in mind?" He inquired.

"Yellow... I think it would be beautiful in yellow."

"Would you call it the Yellow House, Mary?"

"Oh, I don't know... I haven't considered its name."

President Lincoln waited for a few seconds and said calmly, "I think it should remain white, Mary. After all, it is the White House."

"Perhaps you're right, Abe," she said and drifted into a deep slumber.

Lincoln woke up from the fitful sleep to which he was becoming accustomed. The capital city was literally on its last legs. New York's 7th Regiment, as well as forces from other northern states, were on their way to fortify Washington. The pitiful truth of the matter was that they could have marched over the river and occupied the city in less than a day. The President took little solace from the knowledge that his saving grace was probably Jefferson Davis' refusal to believe Washington was so ill-prepared for conflagration.

As he dressed, he heard the familiar footsteps of John Nicolay walking down the long hallway on the second floor. Nicolay lived in a room on the opposite end of the second floor.

"Good morning, John," the President said just as Nicolay rounded the corner of Lincoln's dressing room.

"And the same to you, sir," he replied.

Then, anticipating the President's next question, Nicolay said, "You have a meeting with General Scott at 10:00 a.m. From 11:00 a.m. until 12:30 p.m., we have scheduled fourteen appointments; all office-seekers; looking for your blessing so that they may assist in making the world a better place. Your lunch is scheduled with the Vice President."

Lincoln's Vice President was Hannibal Hamlin of Maine. The two had little in common. But while Hamlin was an avid supporter of the abolitionist cause, he had quickly secured Lincoln's confidence and trust. Lincoln knew that this characteristic made him one of a handful of people in the world with whom Lincoln could speak freely.

"Your afternoon is free, but General McDowell has requested an audience at 3:00 p.m."

"Has he made this request directly?" Lincoln inquired.

"Yes, sir... I do not believe General Scott is aware of McDowell's desire to speak to you privately."

"Well, let's hear what the man has to say," said the President.

Blair House, That Same Day

Irvin McDowell fastened the last button on his General's tunic while gazing with intensity upon his image in the mirror. In fact, his mind was miles away in Richmond. It was just the idea of one American telling the other that he couldn't own one. He didn't need them personally. It wasn't that he minded the Negroes, but many of the families of his West Point classmates did need them. The survival of their agrarian-based business was dependent upon low production costs. Eliminating slavery just didn't make economic sense. But Irvin was a northern man, and he wasn't going to embarrass his family by changing colors. He didn't have to. By staying right where he was, General McDowell would be a much greater asset to the South than he ever would be if he actually declared his allegiance to the cause. Jeff Davis could go on about the noble southern cause, northern yokes, or whatever. To General McDowell, slavery was the poster child for the looming hostilities. Call it what you wish; a southern man didn't need to be told what to do by a yank; full stop. McDowell had been raised in Ohio. That state ended up sending many young men to die for the union cause. This did not mean there weren't sympathies toward the South running throughout the middle and southern part of the state. Based on the duplicitous nature of Irvin McDowell's action, there clearly were.

That afternoon as the President met with General McDowell, a Pinkerton agent approached John Nicolay and advised him that Henry Memminger was in the White House to see him. Nicolay told the guard to admit Henry to his office.

"Hello, old boy," roared Memminger to Nicolay, who rose to greet his old friend.

"Henry, I am surprised to see you here," responded Nicolay.

"Predictability is not a good thing," said Memminger.

"Well, what brings you here? I would have figured you for one who would hunker down in Richmond and watch this mess with amusement while also figuring out ways to profiteer from experience, of course."

17

"John, do give me some credit. Do I look like one who would support efforts to rip our nation asunder?"

"Henry, we know your father's role in the new government. Don't try to pull one over on me. It would probably be best if you make your appearances in Washington few and far between. One of these days, you might find yourself without a return trip."

"John, you are not a very gracious host. Here I come all the way from Richmond to say hello to my old friend, and what do I get in return but a threat," Henry spread his arms out as if in total disbelief.

"I'm sure you are heartbroken," chuckled Nicolay. "Now, what do you really want?"

"Since you insist on inflicting your northern abruptness on me, I will indeed get to the point," said Henry.

"No argument from me," replied John.

"You seem to be doing quite well here, John, living and working in the White House and as a Confidant to the President. I doubt, much goes on that you don't know about...." Nicolay looked impassively upon Henry and did not utter a word.

"So," Memminger continued, "being a student of politics and all things infinitely human, it seemed to me I should visit y'all and see if I can learn what the President is doing about this damned insurrection."

"Who's y'all?" inquired Nicolay.

"You're y'all," responded Memminger.

"How can I be y'all? I'm only me," said Nicolay.

"Sweet Jesus, John. Didn't you learn anything at Harvard? 'Y'all' is singular... 'all y'all' is plural. If I'm talking to you in the singular, you're

18

just y'all."

"Thank you for the clarification," said John. "Now, as regards the information on the President, you must be out of your mind."

"More Yankee rudeness. You know, you are getting gray hair. Is it all work and no play? Nicky, the old boy, are you finding time for any women in your life?"

"Henry, I know what you are on about. I am at something of a loss for words. No doubt in the twentieth century, when an aide to the President feels exasperated because his time is being wasted by an old school chum, he'll think of something else to say besides, 'What do you want?' For now, however, that is the best I can do."

"But I've told you, John. I want information," Henry responded.

"And I've told you. You're dreaming," said John.

Henry grabbed a stool from the corner of the room, positioned it right in front of Nicolay, sat down, and spoke slowly. "John, you know I always felt terrible about that Negro girl's death in our junior year. I mean, it wasn't your fault. It was a mistake. You couldn't be blamed then, and certainly not now. But just the same, do you think President Lincoln can afford to have his right-hand man be someone who might have had a hand, albeit an indirect one, in the death of a pretty young Negro girl? Worse yet, one carrying his child?" Memminger's eyes locked into Nicolay's and froze.

Nicolay returned the frigid stare. After what seemed an eternity, he used the verb instead of the pronoun. "Henry ... you should leave now and be advised that if I see you in Washington, D.C. again, I'll have you arrested."

"Habeas corpus, old boy... you just can't arrest one without cause," deadpanned Memminger.

"Watch that space," Nicolay glared back.

John was one of the few people in America who knew that Lincoln intended to suspend habeas corpus rights in a matter of days.

"If you're not out of here in ten seconds, I'll have you put away now, and you won't see the sun again until this southern issue is resolved.

"So," replied Henry, "what you're really saying is that you would like me to leave. No veni, vidi, vici?"

"Try veni, vidi, cucurri. Now go," the thoroughly irate Nicolay said, still managing to keep his cool.

Memminger took his leave and wasted no time departing the White House grounds. He knew two things he hadn't known a half-hour before. First, his days in Washington were numbered, and second, John Nicolay was indeed a good man. Not even a painful part of Nicolay's past could be used to sway the man's loyalties. Memminger's only regret was that Nicolay was a Yankee.

Still sitting at his desk, Nicolay reflected back on that painful memory he had managed to purge from his conscious mind for the past few years. She had indeed been beautiful. She was a servant working for his college roommate's family. One night all the boys had a bit too much drink. As Nicolay had staggered up to his guest room bed, there she was, folding down the sheets. There was no question the decision to copulate was mutual. No words were spoken. He had noticed her every time he had visited the house. The act was over in five minutes; both parties satiated and excited by the suddenness and satisfaction. She had scurried off, and he had fallen asleep.

A couple of months later, he found her waiting for him in the kitchen pantry. He immediately felt a surge in his loins, but this time, she did not. This time something was wrong. When she told him she was carrying his child, he was speechless. He just didn't know what to do or say, so he stammered something stupid and exited as gracelessly as humanly possible.

Perhaps his biggest mistake was telling his roommate about it. An arrogant Boston Brahmin, his roomie, immediately spread the word that "old Nickie knocked up one of father's niggers." Nicolay was the recipient of more than a little razz from his classmates. No one, however, cared a damn about the girl. Nicolay did, but he didn't know what to do. He knew one thing for sure; he wasn't going over to his roommate's house anytime soon. The roommate told his father. The father summoned the young girl and told her she had one week to be out of his house. Three days later, they fished her out of the Charles River.

"Henry Memminger is a bastard," Nicolay muttered.

"Why would he do that to me?" The light went on simultaneously with the mumbled question.

"My God, he wasn't just being sinister and nosy. He is actually spying for the South. Jesus Christ."

John made a note to dig out a picture of Memminger and turn it over to the army. Shaking the cobwebs loose, he wandered down the hall to see how Lincoln had faired with McDowell.

The White House, April 22, 1861

Oft times, events transpire which seem of little consequence at the time. On April 22, such an event took place. A Massachusetts infantry regiment on its way south was attacked by a band of hooligans, leaving twelve mortally wounded soldiers. Rather than expressing regret, Maryland's governor asked Lincoln to avoid using Maryland for troop movements. A quick glimpse at the map highlighted the absurdity of the request. The Union army had no choice but to traverse Maryland's soil as it assembled in the Washington area for

21

maneuvers and training. The President testily advised all who would listen that if there were ever-another incident in Maryland similar to that which had just transpired, there would be hell to pay. He was taken at his word.

CHAPTER TWO
GERMINATION

Washington, D.C.,
May 1, 1861

"My father doesn't like you. You do know that, don't you?" Kate Chase laughed. She was sitting in the President's office, having set up an appointment through his personal assistant Nicolay.

"Yes, Miss Chase... I know that, and I suppose you do too," Lincoln replied.

"Oh, but I do," she laughed.

"You see, blood is thicker than water, so I must support my father's ambition. Today he is your Secretary of the Treasury. In 1864, he plans to be your President."

"Et tu, Brute," the President muttered aloud.

"Well, Mr. President. I don't know if you know anything about me. The media wags to make me some young lady on the prowl for a husband. I find it amusing. No doubt. I will meet the right man someday, but for now, I would like to focus on making a difference. Ergo, my visit today."

"I'm listening." The President said.

"You have a cabinet full of men. Of course, my father is one of them. Every President since Washington has had cabinets full of men, but I don't doubt that in hundred years, the story will be the same. I'm a realist. However, at the same time, I think I can help you understand women's concerns and their causes. To my knowledge, no President has ever bothered to think about women because we don't vote. But rest assured, Mr. President, women can influence the vote!" She smiled at him.

"Of that, I have no doubt, Miss Chase." He stood and walked over to the window, looking out over the grass in front of the White House. "So, what do you have in mind?"

"I think I can help you as a special advisor on women's affairs. I know. It is unprecedented, but I believe, in my heart, I can make a difference and occasionally guide your thinking on thorny issues that, no offense, men just aren't very good at handling."

Lincoln turned from the window and looked at her. "What does your father think of this?"

"Sir, I didn't discuss this with him. It's not like I am asking you for a paid job. It wouldn't even be a full-time job. I just think I can be of use from time to time, and maybe, just maybe, help our country be the best it can be, particularly in these troubling times."

"Miss Chase," the President responded, "I accept your offer. It is rather unprecedented, but I like the idea of having you as a sounding board. I don't know how often I will need your counsel, but I like your directness. I think you will be a great resource." He stopped and looked at her.

She smiled and took his pause as her cue to leave. They shook hands, and as they did, she had the feeling that he was a good man and he would be true to his word.

Salmon Chase's daughter was the toast of the town. Every eligible bachelor had courted her. She knew she was attractive, and she played the game well, but she hadn't been disingenuous with the President. She really did want to make a difference.

The White House,
May 2, 1881

Slavery was one of the fundamental issues troubling the President throughout his relatively undistinguished congressional and legal career. Lincoln had never come down strongly on either side of the issue. As with most issues of law, he had argued cases on both fronts. In the House of Representatives years before, he quietly supported anti-expansionist legislation, but he never actually spoke against this practice itself.

Washington was not the appropriate venue to avoid this debate. Over 2,000 slaves resided in the capital city, and active trading of newly imported captives took place within miles of the White House. Lincoln knew it well that the war soon to be fought was not directly about the institution of slavery. The seemingly unstoppable train of destruction was fueled by the quest for power. Control was the fundamental goal. Slavery was quite simply becoming the means toward achieving it. The tail was already beginning to wag the dog.

In the not too distant past, Lincoln had actually tried to develop a consensus amongst Whigs and Democrats that the solution to the Negro issue lay in sending all of them back to their native lands. When that idea didn't fly, he resorted to the fence-sitting position with which he seemed most comfortable. Even so, as he paced the floor of his office on this beautiful spring day, he knew there were few men in the country who understood the strength of his hand better if he chose to play the slavery card.

The White House,
May 13, 1881

It was 7:30 AM, and Lincoln found himself back in the squeaking chair, tilting slightly to the left, as he leaned forward to write. Before this, he read various military manuals and accounts of victorious campaigns dating back to the early eighteenth century. While he boiled internally every time some effete east coast snob referred to him as a hayseed, he readily acknowledged to himself that he was anything but an expert in military affairs. He meant to rectify that situation, and his first step was to study military history enough to be able to detect trends and patterns which led to decisive victories. The next two and half hours would fly by as the President was wholly absorbed by Wellington's account of the Battle of Waterloo.

General Scott appeared with Nicolay precisely at 10:00 AM, as scheduled. His last formal meeting with Lincoln had been more than a month ago. The President was expecting a report which confirmed tremendous progress in military readiness. Nicolay showed the way to General into Lincoln's office and discreetly disappeared. Nicolay's ability to appear and disappear at exactly the right time was one of his endearing qualities. What very few visitors to the White House knew was that Nicolay's office, which was adjacent to Lincoln's, had a small glass panel through which he could see Lincoln and whoever was present inside. Nicolay read Lincoln like a book. By watching his boss, he knew exactly when to enter his office and conjure up the appropriate words to ensure a swift termination of the meeting at hand.

"How good to see you, General." Lincoln offered his hand to the nation's senior ranking general.

"How are you?"

"Well, as can be, Mr. President, for an old man with gout and an overwhelming level of despondency over the present situation," Scott responded with a gravelly voice for which stage actors would have killed.

Lincoln pondered over Scott's response to a question that hadn't been asked.

"Well, General, nevertheless, it is a pleasure to have your presence in situ. It's been too long. Your visits do wonders to cheer me up," Lincoln mused, thinking to himself that most of the cheer was derived from the fact that Scott was so totally self-absorbed that the conversation always took amusing and unpredictable turns.

"I beg your pardon, Sir. I meant not to cast a gloomy cloud over the White House."

The General spoke in a borderline mockingly deferential tone. General Scott was similar to many members of Lincoln's cabinet in at least one respect; he had run (unsuccessfully) for President in 1852. Lincoln was surrounded by people who would have loved to be President. However, the simple truth of the matter was that only he, Abraham Lincoln, actually was President!

"No offense taken, General. But on to matters of import, how goes the troop readiness effort? How soon can we move on the secessionist states?"

"Sir," Scott replied, "we don't even have an army yet. I can't tell you when we can launch an offensive strike against the enemy."

Scott hesitated and then said with calculated precision, "My best guess is that we will not be able to move until next January, at the earliest."

The General knew that if looks could kill, he would be dead then and there on the spot. Inwardly, his pulse picked up its pace. Outwardly, he maintained his composure. He was a decorated war hero. The woodchopper from Illinois would not intimidate General Winfield Scott.

"General," Lincoln paused, scratching the stubble on his chin, actually turning away from the General and then looking out the window, he continued, "Your response is most unsatisfactory. Every day we delay, we allow a weaker enemy to build its strength. This is

27

folly. Surely you, as our ranking military officer, would agree that delay is counterproductive. We need to strike General, and we need to do so as soon as possible. I think, Sir, it is time we appoint a field general, reporting to you, of course, but someone ready to equip, train, and move our army into the field post haste."

Scott sat impassively for at least ten seconds. He inhaled and exhaled deeply. Lincoln turned to face him and couldn't help but notice the tiny fleck of spittle stuck in the corner of Scott's mouth. Every time he exhaled, a small bubble formed.

"Mr. President, you are our constitutional commander in chief. I am here as your servant. But with all due respect, sir, you are out of your depth. Precipitous action on our part would produce calamitous results. Begging your pardon, sir, but if I may be so bold as you suggest…well…let's say from a political viewpoint, it would behoove this administration to make sure that our first foray into battle results in a decisive victory. Any other result will cause your most ardent and fervent supporters to run from you like a slave man from a noose."

Lincoln frowned at Scott.

"Oh, begging the expression, Sir," Scott said without much conviction.

Lincoln dismissed Scott's slur with a wave of his hand. The comment actually triggered a diversionary thought process.

"You know, General, during the election, I proposed a tax referendum aimed at raising enough funds from all Untied States to free the Negro and pay for his return to his tribal land. No one seemed interested."

Lincoln finally swiveled around and faced the General. In addition to the spittle issue, the bulbous veins dotting Scott's face repulsed Lincoln. He was convinced Winfield Scott was set to topple over any day. Lincoln wondered how many porters would be required to haul the carcass out of his office. Then he realized Mary had put a new rug down in his office. If Scott died at that moment, the porters would have to make the work of body removal fast, or Scott's body would purge its fluids and ruin the new rug. Lincoln did not need the hassle of Mary's inevitable harangue over the soiled needlepoint rug.

Scott saw Lincoln staring in his direction but couldn't for the life of him figure out what the President was thinking. Shifting his weight from one side of his massive buttocks to the other, Scott interjected,

"Mr. President...not to push the subject, but one must consider what the jackals in today's free press would do to you if the first Union army thrust against the south is anything but a major victory. Horace Greeley up in New York would have a field day at your expense."

Scott stopped to see if his ploy was having any impact.

Lincoln was still not on his side. Damn the man. Didn't he care about what the press said? What about his popularity? Could he and would he keep pushing for early action?

"General," began Lincoln, "had I spent my adult life heeding the advice of members of the free press, I would this moment be a mere gangly log splitter in Illinois. No, sir, we cannot wait until next year for an offensive. I am relying on you to expedite this situation. More importantly, I am surprised you didn't take me up on my suggestion just minutes ago that we should nominate a field commander. General Scott, I would prefer it to be a suggestion rather than an order, but that, Sir, is up to you."

Scott sighed, took a deep breath, and said, "Well, if you insist, Mr. President. I would suggest the commander be Irvin McDowell".

Abe Lincoln smiled and responded, "This comes as no surprise to me. In fact, I took the liberty of drawing up the paperwork to commission him as a Brigadier General. Lest things seem too hasty, we'll wait a couple of weeks and then name him leader of the Army of Northeastern Virginia. It will fall to you two to get us ready for action. I know I am repeating myself, but every day that passes is a day that helps General Lee."

President Lincoln paused and then continued, "Do you know, General Scott, that on the same day you visited me last month, I received General McDowell a few hours later?"

General Scott grunted, indicating this was news to him.

"I would say he lobbied hard for the job he is about to get, but his very presence indicated he wasn't too sure you would be his advocate. Well, I guess all's well that ends well, heh?"

General Scott nodded begrudgingly and said, "I will get to work on this, Mr. President, and no doubt will see you soon."

As he began the arduous process of removing himself from his chair, Nicolay appeared to escort him out.

Lincoln bid Scott adieu, waited for him to plod downstairs, and then proceeded to secure his stovepipe hat and head for some fresh air.

"Tell the job grubbers they'll have to wait," Lincoln said as he passed John Nicolay returning to his desk.

Little did he know that he had just aligned the two forces of ill will to ensure that the painfully slow Union preparation process would continue. Ironically, Generals Scott and McDowell were equally unaware of each other's treachery.

The business of war was perplexing. He was spending what seemed like every spare moment studying military tactics and proven strategies. He knew the law of large numbers was on his side. He felt in his gut that a well-orchestrated "crab thrust" into Virginia could end hostilities before they really even began. The crab thrust was his nomenclature. He hadn't found it referenced in any military book.

Time and again throughout history, the victors have emerged from a decisive battle by way of superior manpower, weaponry, supplies, and strategy. The North had the upper hand in manpower, weaponry, and supplies. In Lincoln's view, the army needed to locate the hub of the southern army's strength and move on it as would a crab do to its prey; two menacing claws surrounding the target, followed by a massive infrastructure at the front of which was the mouth. The claws would envelop the enemy and drive it into the mouth of the union army.

Nodding to the Pinkerton guard at the West Entrance, the President slipped around back to the South Lawn. For all the intrigue of the capital city, it was always remarkably serene on the lawn. Lincoln gathered his thoughts. Several things troubled him. Never before had he encountered so many people who appeared to place their personal agendas ahead of all other concerns. This was a time of crisis. Was he the only elected official in Washington who cared? The city was beginning to teem with blue-coated soldiers. Yet, according to his cabinet, the military was still woefully ill-prepared for combat. Then there was the issue of Generals Scott and McDowell. McDowell was Scott's choice as senior ranking field commander. Scott, riddled with gout and unable to even mount a horse, would not be commanding anybody anywhere. McDowell did not, it seemed, even talk much to Scott; very odd. It was upon McDowell's shoulders that the burden of attack would probably be placed. That was all well and good, but for one minor issue; both Generals were advocating interminable delay. It was driving Lincoln to the brink. He was beside himself with frustration, but at least the McDowell ascension was now on the table and in the works.

The President found a cherry tree that had long since shed its spring flowers. Having sat down against the solid trunk, he noticed a solitary dandelion standing upright, as would a vigilant sentinel. He broke the stem off at the base and studied the yellow flower.

"Soon, you will age and turn white," he muttered, "but the wind will blow, and you will spread your seed across this great lawn."

It occurred to him that many men would like to live the dandelion's life. "The dandelion lives its life in reverse order to man." He meticulously picked the yellow pieces of the flower off the stem one by one and threw them on the lawn.

"There, now you will have your chance, and you will have it before you turn gray."

The irony (albeit an abstract irony of the type which could cause Lincoln to ponder while leaving most others baffled) hit home. His two top generals were asking him to be a dandelion. They wanted the army to turn from yellow to gray before sowing its seed. Where, by Jesus, in any of the annals of military history did this strategy pay off? Preparation was one thing, but to miss the moment of opportunity was unpardonable. He was on his feet, pacing back and forth without even being conscious that he had left the ground.

"It's like eating lamb without mint jelly, for God's sake. Why do I feel so alone?"

"Abraham," a voice penetrated the fog enveloping his thoughts.

"Abe Lincoln…" It was Mary, calling from the White House. "Come to lunch. Horace Greeley is joining us." The words sunk in. Lincoln grimaced and wondered how John Nicolay let this one fall through the cracks.

Just as he completed that thought, Nicolay appeared and jogged out to the President. "I know," he said before Lincoln even opened his mouth.

"Sir, Mrs. Lincoln told me two weeks ago the fashion editor from the New York Herald would be in for lunch today. That seemed harmless enough. And, in point of fact, he's here, Sir. Unfortunately, he is accompanied by Mr. Greeley."

Lincoln, whose hat was in hand, straightened up, placed it on his head, and strode toward his luncheon destiny.

"Consider it a lesson learned, John." Lincoln disappeared inside the White House.

The White House, May 24, 1861

Abe Lincoln sat back in his office chair, an old desk chair converted by a handy White House carpenter into a rocking chair. The spring squeaked no matter how still the president tried to sit. The fact was he didn't sit still all that often. Lincoln was a squirmer. It always seemed to him that there was too much to be done while being away sitting in one place. The problem with his present capacity was that he wasn't sure if sitting immobile in his chair wasn't the best way to ensure that nothing catastrophic occurred under his watch.

While his face never exactly portrayed the look of one who has achieved bliss in all matters, Lincoln's furrowed brow indicated something was amiss. Indeed, John Nicolay had just brought him the news he didn't want to hear. Virginia had just the day before joined the confederate states. The vote was 132,201 to 37,451. It was clear that Virginians did not want to be told what to do. After the vote, Lincoln had immediately ordered Colonel Elmer Ellsworth, a confidant, and friend, to lead a brigade into Alexandria and secure the town. The mission was readily accomplished, but in his zeal to replace the confederate flag flying over a town center hotel with the Stars and Stripes, Colonel Ellsworth was ambushed and killed. Lincoln had no way of knowing, as he sat there that afternoon of May 24, that he was experiencing a sense of loss to which he would have to become numb over the next four years. Shortly before his death in 1865, he remarked to various family members that he was sure his heart had ceased to exist; so many times, it had been ripped apart by grief.

General McDowell would officially take on leadership responsibilities in a couple of days. It couldn't come soon enough. Lincoln had requested his presence later this day at the White House. The President prayed McDowell's new role would unleash a more aggressive man.

He stared at the newspaper on his desk. Apparently, his concerns about Horace Greeley had not been unjustified. There was a cartoon depicting him as a baboon.

"That caricature certainly does a disservice to that poor baboon," he chuckled.

Not that long after, Mr. Greeley wrote, "…if this country is destined to fall, history will lay the blame on Abraham Lincoln and his cabinet, with the half-hearted commanders of the forces…."

Abe Lincoln's guts were right. Horace Greeley, the famed newsman from New York, was no friend.

Across Town,
May 24, 1861

George McClellan tucked his napkin into his star-studded navy-blue general's tunic and dove into the turnip soup which had just been placed in front of him. His posture was rigid, to say the least. General McClellan did everything by the book. He had studied every military leader ever known to man. If history led one to conclude that all great generals walked with a limp and stuttered, the good general would immediately adopt a gimp and stammer. He was utterly devoid of creative thought, yet here he was, poised to replace General McDowell the moment he stumbled. McDowell had only been promoted ten days earlier, and even though McClellan had been made Commander of the Ohio front a couple of weeks before, he knew in his heart he was about to be given the top job. He was convinced it would not be long before McDowell's incompetence was manifested. The stumble would happen because the man was wholly useless! McClellan was utterly convinced of his intellectual and leadership superiority over McDowell. His ascent to supreme commander of the Union army was not a question of if but rather when. Besides, he was holding an ace in his deck. Secretary of the Treasury Salmon Chase was a huge supporter and was already whispering in Lincoln's ear.

The White House, May 24, 1861

Later that same day, John Nicolay led General McDowell up the circular stairs to the living quarters, down the hall, and into Lincoln's office. The office was not far down on the right-hand side of the hallway. People today marvel at the stately White House, but it wasn't always that way. In spite of Mary's efforts to spend considerable amounts of money to spruce it up, the Lincolns had moved into a house that was "deplorably shabby" (according to Mary's first cousin, Lizzie Grimsley.) It was, however, just fine for the President. As he put it, the White House was "furnished well enough when (we) came (and it was) better than any house (we) had ever lived in." Perhaps more humorously (morose humor perhaps, given Mary's out-of-control spending), the President noted that no one needed to incur more expenses to add "flub dubs for that damned old house!"

But we digress. The purpose of the meeting on May 24 was to review General McDowell's first steps upon appointment as the army's (de facto) leader. General Scott had been invited to attend but had sent word that massive roast beef and copious amounts of port wine had become stuck in his toes, and he was presently immobile. Well, that was not exactly the message. It was something more like that he was experiencing another round of severely debilitating gout and was unable to leave his residence.

General McDowell and the President exchanged greetings, and Lincoln wasted no time. "General, I am so looking forward to your assuming command. Tell me, have you and General Scott visited and drawn up a preparedness timeline?"

"Mr. President," the General responded, "First, I would like to thank you for giving me the opportunity to lead our troops. I feel that with the proper amount of time, the outcome of the pending troubles will become a foregone conclusion".

The President looked long and hard at Irvin McDowell and said, "General, allow me a question."

General McDowell nodded agreeably as though Old Abe needed his permission to continue. "When you say 'with the proper amount of time,' we can win this war. What exactly is that? One month, six months, one year, five years? Do you get my point here?"

General McDowell shifted in his chair and crossed his right leg over his left. The President noticed that he had moved one leg over the other no fewer than ten times in the short time they had been speaking. He thought it was all rather strange, and McDowell must be very nervous, but he pushed that thought away as he realized he could easily find himself going down some analytic rabbit hole and not even listen to the General's answer. As an aside, the reader should know that Abraham Lincoln's mind never stopped. It was constantly churning, whether awake or asleep. It went places other minds did not go. To some, it was a blessing, but to others, a curse. Lincoln was not sure where he fell along that line. All he knew at that very moment in time was that he needed to refocus on the situation at hand.

"Well, sir, given the fact that June is nigh upon us, I would say the proper and absolute minimum amount of time we'll need, in this context, is seven months. We cannot possibly ready an army for an attack upon General Lee's Virginia troops in a shorter period of time."

Lincoln was incredulous. He closed his eyes and rubbed them, and while seeing stars, from the pressure he placed upon his pupils, he convinced himself that when his eyes reopened, they would see Winfield Scott. There was no way he was hearing another military leader lobby for an interminable delay! Alas, he opened his eyes, and there before him sat Irvin McDowell. At that moment, the general re-crossed his legs.

"General, I have made my intentions clear from the moment the secesh states chose to go their own way. I have been told I am out of my depth, that I do not understand the complexities of warfare. At first blush, one would have to agree. Heavens to Betsy, I would have to agree! But General, I am no longer a Lincoln war knowledge doubter. Indeed, I am beginning to believe I may understand the art of war better than any of my generals!"

Irvin McDowell sat up in his chair, crossed his right leg over his left, and then his left leg over his right, and was about to speak. Lincoln had counted close to twenty leg crosses by that time and was very amused. Or was he amazed? He pondered that for a brief moment and then continued. "General, have you read the 'Art of War?"

General McDowell's expression made it clear that not only had he not read the book, but he had no idea what it was.

"I see," said Lincoln. "It was written in the 5th century BC by a Chinese military man named Sun Tzu. I recommend it to you. In fact, I will see to it that all my Generals are given a copy. Read it, General. And do come back to me and tell me your views on the importance of military intelligence and rapid preparedness."

McDowell felt as though he was in a virtual boxing ring and taking repeated hits. He gathered his senses and told the President he would be pleased to read the book and report back with his take-aways.

The President had begun to become known for making it clear that his meetings were over. This session proved to be no exception. Lincoln stood and walked over to the General, who was just rising from his chair. As McDowell looked up to this approaching man, some 6 inches taller than him, the sunlight came through the office window and cast such light on Lincoln's face that all time momentarily stopped for the General. He wasn't sure what it was, but it was something of an other-worldly look, and it put McDowell off his game. Lincoln grabbed his hand and shook it firmly.

"General, let me be very clear. Seven months is unacceptable. I want to be in the field in no more than two months. I want a decisive victory, and I don't ever want to look back. I am counting on you. I am tired of the 'why-nots.' I only want to hear about how we are going to accomplish our goal. No more why not; only how. Do we understand each other?"

McDowell shook himself from the temporary trance into which he had fallen after seeing Lincoln's sun-draped face.

"Yes, Sir," was all he said.

And then he took his leave. McDowell walked down the hall and downstairs to the ground floor of the White House. There were various people milling around. He didn't know any of them, but then again, he could have walked past his brother and not recognized him. His mind was on one thing. The President had ordered him into the field before the end of July. This news would come as a shock to Jefferson Davis. As he walked out the door onto the south lawn, he suddenly realized the President had given him a massive opportunity. Yes, lives would be lost. He grinned as it had just dawned on him that he could almost single-handedly ensure that the union army walked into a bloody mess when that day arrived when the north met the south on the battlefield.

CHAPTER THREE
ROOTS OF MANASSAS

Richmond, Virginia,
June 7, 1861

The library inside the large Brownstone-style house in the Court End area of Richmond that was occupied by Jefferson Davis and his staff had become the equivalent of Lincoln's second-floor White House office. Davis understood how the military and government should operate. He had been President Franklin Pierce's Secretary of War during the Pierce administration in the years 1853-1857. He had also served in the House and Senate. His first wife (who died of malaria) was President Zachary Taylor's daughter. Jeff Davis, in short, had a pedigree.

When all was said and done immediately after the war, the second-guessers said Jeff Davis would not relinquish control, and his tendency to keep the information tight and only talk to his inner circle led to many southern defeats. Fair or not, when he thought about putting his first cabinet together, among others, he first turned to Robert Toombs of Georgia to be his Secretary of State, Christopher Memminger of South Carolina to be his Treasury leader, and LeRoy Pope Walker to be his Secretary of War.

It was this group of men that Henry Memminger saw when he entered the library.

"Father," Henry said, nodding in his father's direction. "President Davis, Gentlemen, it is nice to see you all."

Leroy Pope Walker looked at Christopher Memminger's son and said, "Lordy, Lordy, I haven't seen you since you were knee-high to a grasshopper. It's good to see you, son."

President Davis interrupted the niceties. "Henry, your timing is good. Things are heating up, and it appears that action is taking place faster than I had been assured by you and other sources." (Henry knew the "other sources" probably meant General McDowell, but he also knew that he wasn't supposed to know that the General was playing on both sides of the fence.)

"Six days ago, our troops skirmished with the yanks at the Fairfax Court House, and four days ago, George McClellan surprised our boys in the western part of this state. I can tell that General Butler is approaching the garrison that we have in Little Bethal, so I imagine we will have more action in the next few days." (Davis was right. But if anything would happen, the battle there portended things to come. The union army was meant to surprise the confederates, but it instead fired on itself, thus alerting the grey coats to its presence. The result was an outcome with more federal troops dead than their opponents.)

"Henry," Jeff Davis continued, "Do you bring us any news as to what is happening in Washington? We have been operating on the basis that we would have months to organize our troops and battle plan accordingly."

Henry was older than his years, notwithstanding his rather despicable attempt to pull John Nicolay into the abyss of governmental double-crossing. He was honest, focused, and intelligent and regarded his reference to the unfortunate slave girl in Boston. He wasn't proud of what he did, but he knew that desperate times call for desperate measures. "Sir, the news is not good, but perhaps there is a silver lining." His opening comment was greeted by a chorus of furrowed brows. Clearly, the stage was his to explain. "As you know, General Scott has all but been sidelined." He paused and looked directly at President Davis. "Sir, may I speak freely?" David nodded in assent. Henry was not sure if the other cabinet members (including-for that matter-his father) were fully briefed on his activities. "General Scott was an invaluable source for me. While he is the titular head, Generals like McDowell, McClellan, and Butler are off and running. I am sure that they give lip service to General Scott, but for all intents and purposes, he is now a spectator. To put it bluntly, his value as an asset has diminished."

Henry continued, "Now to General McDowell…" Henry knew he had to tread softly, throw out some bait, and if President Davis bit, then the conversation could continue. "As you know, he has taken on responsibility for their Virginia operations. It seems clear that Virginia is the first staging ground for this conflagration, and the skirmishes of the past week would seem to back that up. There are rumors, Sir, that General McDowell may have sympathies that lean toward Richmond. I am told by someone I trust that President Lincoln has made it very clear that he expects significant advancement in the field before the end of July. Perhaps there is an opportunity in what seems to be an otherwise uncomfortable turn of events." Henry stopped and looked at the gentlemen sitting around the table. He had been standing the entire time.

"Henry, why don't you sit down and join us?" said President Davis. Henry sat in an empty chair next to his father. "You are quite right, Henry. Lincoln's eagerness for action is a spanner in works. But you are amazingly prescient, or whatever you may be, I don't actually know", he chuckled, looking across the table at Henry, and then went on, "regarding General McDowell. You see, he is in our camp. Lincoln could not have chosen more wisely. I guess, to be fair, McDowell is General Scott's parting gift to us. We now have our man leading the army. In a perfect world, he can lead the Union into our arms, and we can deliver a decisive blow before this war turns into a long and ugly sojourn."

Henry feigned ignorance and said, "That is quite remarkable. It seems God must be on our side. Now we just need to make sure we do not disappoint God."

"Quite right, son," said Christopher Memminger. "Now, what would

41

be very useful is to know what General McDowell's plans are, so we can set the trap. We need to know when, where, how many, all battle formations, and their strategy. That's not too much to ask, is it?" His father smiled, letting Henry know that the question was rhetorical. Leroy Pope Walker shifted in his seat, laughed, and said, "Well, Chris, maybe you should be Secretary of War, and I should run Treasury!" Everyone around the table smiled.

Henry was excused shortly thereafter. He walked around the streets of Court End. The trees were now in full bloom, and it was not yet hot and muggy as it would be in July and August. Richmond was a wonderful town. Henry had been born in South Carolina but attended the University of Virginia for his business degree, having obtained his undergraduate diploma at Harvard. He made many fast friends during those two years in Charlottesville, and settling in Richmond had seemed second nature to him. Little had he known that a few years later, his adopted town would become home to the Confederacy. He had quite the challenge on his hands. After last month's meeting with Nicolay, he had to assume he was on northern security watch lists. That notwithstanding, it was incumbent upon him to return to the Capital and see what he could ascertain about upcoming battle plans.

Jefferson, Davis - President of the Confederate States

As mentioned before, Kate Chase was the woman "about town." Let me be clear. She was a highly respected young lady. A German American named Carl Schurz said of her, "She was about eighteen years old, tall and slender and exceptionally well-formed…Her little nose… fitted pleasingly into her face … at the same time with vivacious hazel eyes, shaded by long dark lashes and arched-over by proud eyebrows."

Is it possible to imagine a woman in the twenty-first century being described in such terms? Allow me to answer for you. The answer is "no." But we are focusing on the mid-19th century; you know, a time when one could describe the indescribable and do so without fear of reprisal. In short, Kate Chase was a very good-looking, perspicacious woman. She knew who she was, where she was, and that she was intrigued by the log splitter from Illinois. She was the Secretary of Treasury's daughter and was being courted by several eligible bachelors. In time, she would marry Governor William Sprague of Rhode Island. That time, such as it was, was two years later. She enjoyed being courted and the social life in the nation's capital. She also relished the fact that she had a unique role as a counselor to the President. She took it seriously.

On this cool June day, she had her first advisory conversation with the President. They met in Lafayette Square, just outside the White House. A bench sat discretely on some grass and bushes between the White House and what would (similarly) one day be the Hay-Adams Hotel. There are several points to be made. Lafayette Square would, in the twenty-first century, become a focal point for protest. By that time, Americans had forgotten the blood, sweat, and tears that had been shed to preserve the Union and the freedoms that came along with it.

The Hay-Adams did not yet exist. There were palatial homes at the time, and it would ensure that these homes were ultimately purchased and razed. The Hay Adams Hotel was, after some economic turmoil, finally opened in 1932. The story gets more interesting from here. John Hay was a great friend of John Nicolay. Hay was actually Lincoln's deputy personal assistant, providing assistance to Nicolay in his quest to serve the President, day in and day out. After the dust had settled and the public began to digest the amazing accomplishments of Abraham Lincoln, Nicolay and Hay collaborated on a book entitled "Abraham Lincoln: A History." It was a best seller. But once again, that is the future, and we are here to discuss them here and now.

The President was punctual, as was Kate. They arrived within thirty seconds of each other. It was odd that Lincoln felt a sense of familiarity with this bold (maybe even brash, he wondered) young lady. She just had an easy-going way about her.

"How are you, Mr. Lincoln?" Kate inquired, "Is General McDowell making any progress?" She laughed, "I mean, there are thousands of blue troops parading up and down our boulevards. If wars were parades, surely we would win handily."

He decided brash was a suitable adjective. Lincoln chuckled and said, "Indeed, Miss Chase. Alas, I suspect you know as well as I that the rebs could care less how pretty our troops are and how nicely they march in straight lines. Of all nations, did we not invent the new-age art of warfare? We taught the British a lesson, not once but twice. War is an ugly business - blood, bones, mangled bodies, death, and agony. There is no joy. Yet as I read the papers, I see how little our media has learned from the past. It's as though they think we are going to have a big picnic when that day arrives that we move our troops toward General Johnston's in Virginia. I am at a complete loss for words to describe my frustration with all I see."

Kate asked him when he thought we would engage the enemy. Lincoln looked off into the distance and replied, "I am pushing

General McDowell to take action by mid-July. We shall see, Kate. We shall see."

They ended up talking for an hour or so, and ironically, she never got around to discussing the women's suffrage issues she came to address. They talked about the war, and Lincoln found it refreshing to hear a young person's views.

Irvin McDowell's Residence, June 15, 1862

It was 11 PM, and Generals McDowell, McClellan, and Scott had withdrawn from the dining room and were enjoying cigars in McDowell's parlor. This was McDowell's home office. In addition to a large four-legged desk with a comfortable-looking chair, the room had a fireplace, a brown leather couch, and two matching brown leather chairs. It was a comfortable room, so much that it would have been odd not to have enjoyed a cigar and glass of port in there with some regularity!

The evening had come about for two reasons; McDowell decided he needed to make at least a cursory effort to make General Scott feel needed, and also because he knew George McClellan coveted his job. McClellan was a threat, so McDowell took a page out of Lincoln's book and decided it was in his best interest to keep McClellan close enough to him that he could not operate with impunity to McDowell's detriment. McDowell had many faults, but he wasn't a fool. So for these reasons, he had hosted a very nice dinner that exceeded his expectations in many ways.

General Scott had plopped himself down in one of the nice leather chairs by the fireplace. It was June in Washington, so no fire was lit there, but Scott was nonetheless in a full sweat. He had overeaten (no surprise) and over-consumed his beverages. McDowell was a bit of a red Bordeaux fan and had served some nice clarets. The three of them had consumed four bottles over the course of dinner and were now well into a bottle of port. Winfield Scott could already feel the prickly tentacles of gout attacking his toes. He knew that by morning he would likely not be able to move. So be it; the morning was still hours away, and there was port to be drunk!

While there was no love lost between McDowell and McClellan, they knew they needed each other if the army was going to succeed. However, George McClellan had no idea he was sitting with two gentlemen who had goals that were very different than his. The irony was that McClellan's own ego would ultimately prove to be as much of a menace to Lincoln's plans for a quick and decisive victory as would McDowell's double dealings. There were many ways to skin the Union's cat: some overt, and some covert; some intentional, and some simply borne of narcissistic incompetence. All of those attributes were found in this room that night.

McDowell topped off their glasses and sat down on the couch. "So, I think it is safe to say that the 3 of us agree we are being pushed into combat far too early. The log-splitter is not a military man, although he certainly fancies himself to be an expert! Our troops are green. But the President wants action, so action he will get. I am aiming to be in the field taking on Johnston and his Virginia corps by mid-July."

"Preposterous!" said McClellan. "We need the rest of this year to prepare for war."

Irvin McDowell shook his head. "George, we have been over this subject countless times. Yes, what we need is time, but that is not a luxury we have. The Commander in Chief demands action. It is incumbent upon us to deliver action. Now, we know the rebs are in the same position. Except we are actually better supplied on all fronts. We have the northern military-industrial complex behind us and the New England states lining up all the supplies we need. The rebs are discombobulated, and their railways use a different gauge, thus limiting their ability to get supplies as far north as they need. In spite of all our challenges, we are in a superior position. No, we will do the President's bidding. We will prepare to move, and as we discussed at dinner, it would appear Manassas is the logical first step in this conquest."

Scott grunted. The other two were not sure if it was in affirmation or just a spontaneous noise. Upon closer inspection, they were amused to see that it was actually a snore. General Scott was fast asleep.

"Well, I suppose the General is giving me my cue to leave," chuckled McClellan. He rose, as did McDowell. Scott continued to snore.

"Do me a favor and send his driver in to fetch him, would you?" McDowell asked George McClellan as the General found his hat and headed for the door. General Scott's carriage was outside, and his very large Negro driver was quite accustomed to gathering the General from various positions of repose and getting him safely home.

The White House,
June 26, 1861

Lincoln had spent the last couple of weeks meeting with cabinet members and the endless parade of job seekers. The role of the President evolved greatly over the next century and a half, but in the mid-nineteenth century, the President was amazingly accessible and, well, as Abe Lincoln said to Nicolay one afternoon, "I believe every Tom, Dick, and Harry in the US has been in this House looking for a job!"

Abe was satisfied that his pep talk a couple of months back had stirred his cabinet into action. The war machine was kicking into gear. It wasn't easy. In fact, it was very difficult to recruit troops. Many states had resorted to a limited one-hundred-day draft. They sold inductees on the notion of a very quick, decisive campaign that would take a little over three months, and then they could go home. This was yet another reason why Lincoln needed to see his troops doing more than just parading around Washington.

Also, on this day, Horace Greeley's New York Tribune printed an article stating that the Confederate Congress was planning to assemble in Richmond on July 20th. Greeley suggested that would be impossible, for surely the war would be over by then, and the Union army would have occupied Richmond. Lincoln wasn't sure about that, but the sentiment spread like wildfire, and that did help his push for action. The public clearly wanted this venture over and done with.

The President sat in his office staring out at the green space below. Tennessee had voted to secede. Lincoln was nonetheless pondering ways to recruit troops from that state and would, in fact, announce a few days later that a campaign would be launched to give young men in Tennessee a choice of which side to join. These were indeed strange and trying times!

Washington, D.C.
July 3, 1861

States in the North were preparing to celebrate Independence Day. In Boston, elaborate plans were underway to enjoy a day full of festivities. J.L.C. Amee, Boston Chief of Police, sent a note to all citizens. In it, he said, "Police arrangements will be made to prevent discharge of firearms, squibs, crackers, mock processions, the blowing of horns, and other annoyances. Every facility will be extended by the Government for the rational enjoyment of the festivities of the day." Bostonians would celebrate, but they would do so under the guidance of the authorities!

Closer to home, the President had bigger fish to fry. In a few days, the rebel army had inched closer to the nation's capital. Just under 20,000 southern troops had quietly positioned themselves less than ten miles from Washington. McDowell sent General John Fremont out with an equal number of troops with the intention of dissuading the grey coats from venturing any closer. The tactic succeeded. The rebels backed off. This told Lincoln that the enemy wasn't ready either.

Lincoln's principal task on this day was to prepare his remarks for the imminent July 4th celebration in Washington. He was well aware of the irony that several states would not be recognizing it as Independence Day, and it saddened him. He resolved to make a strong speech about the absolute indivisibility of the Union. This speech and the build-up to the first major battle had both intended and unintended consequences. The President intended to motivate his base. In this, he succeeded. But in so doing, he also made it nigh impossible to walk back from his position, and that made any kind of peace with Jefferson Davis virtually impossible. The course was set. The only unknown was the outcome.

Independence Day also marked the beginning of an extraordinary session for the Senate. The President had called them back to address the pressing matters at hand. The daily, mundane work of the government, after all, had to continue. They actually accomplished several legislative feats, but the most difficult decision came a week later when they expelled their southern brethren from the Senate. There was no going back.

Concurrent with President Lincoln's preparation of July 4 remarks, Henry Memminger had slipped back into D.C. He had the advantage of not standing out; there were thousands of young men in the city. Alas, the vast majority of them were wearing blue uniforms. Memminger had solved that problem by acquiring an army lieutenant's uniform. He actually cut quite a dashing figure.

In the days subsequent to his meeting in Richmond, Memminger had decided on a strategy to pursue his goals. After some deliberation, he determined that the best way to be able to report back to Jeff Davis regarding General McDowell's battle plan was to go straight to the horse's mouth. With his pristine, pressed blue uniform donned and ready for action, Henry Memminger waited for General McDowell to return home for lunch after the AM parade drills. He had his lines down. As the General started to walk the steps to his brick house, Henry scooted up behind him and said, "General!"

McDowell turned around and looked at the young Lieutenant inquisitively. "Sir," said Memminger, "I am Henry Memminger, and I have a message from John Nicolay and would truly appreciate a few moments of your time." In one line, he told the truth and lied. He was indeed Henry Memminger, but he certainly was not there on behalf of John Nicolay. Unbeknownst to Nicolay was that he had managed to help Memminger after all. His name was indeed a door opener.

"Of course, Lieutenant. Come in." He walked up the stairs, opened the door, and entered. Pointing to the same study where he had recently witnessed General Scott fall fast asleep after dinner, he said, "Have a seat in there. I am going to freshen up and will be back shortly."

Memminger responded with a "Yes, sir" and disappeared into McDowell's office.

The General's office was full not only of books but several oil paintings. Washington, Jefferson, and (John) Adams were on the walls. His bases were covered, albeit the preference appeared to lean toward a proclivity favoring federal more than states' rights; that is, if anyone can possibly infer another's proclivities based on paintings.

"Well, Lieutenant, what can I do for Mr. Nicolay?" McDowell began the sentence as he rounded the corner and entered the study. He had a hand towel and was drying his hands. Throwing the towel on the back of his leather couch, he sat down and faced Memminger, who had chosen General Scott's preferred chair.

"Sir, allow me to begin by saying I'm sorry to have employed subterfuge a few minutes ago. I am indeed Henry Memminger, but in point of fact, John Nicolay did not send me to see you. And, begging your pardon, Sir, but while you and I were not introduced, we did actually see each other some time ago during a certain meeting in Richmond."

McDowell employed his trademarked leg crossing shift and stared intently into Henry's eyes. "Alright then. Why are you here?"

"Sir, I come from Jefferson Davis. You and I are aligned, if I may be so bold. The President needs to know how you plan to advance the cause of the South. With what would appear to be battle lines drawn and contact with the enemy drawing nigh, we, ummm, President Davis is anxious to have every possible advantage." Memminger paused and looked McDowell in the eyes.

The General stared intently back at him. He had a choice to make. In times of war, it was not unknown for leaders to test their military command. Genghis Khan had been known to routinely test his inner circle. Those who failed the test did not see the next sunrise. It was certainly one way of ensuring loyal subjects. A century and a half later, from this particular conversation, a young overweight leader in a country ultimately known as North Korea would employ the same tactics. Some things never change.

"I assume I should call you Henry, then, as it is unlikely that you are a Lieutenant in my army?" McDowell asked. Memminger nodded affirmatively. "Your name is indeed familiar to me. You are Christopher's son?"

"Yes, Sir, you were present in a meeting one time when I briefed President Davis."

"Ha! Well, these are tricky times. You really are who and what you say you are then, Good heavens. What a strange world in which we live, heh?" The General leaned back into the couch, re-crossed his legs, and then uncrossed them, leaped up, and walked over to a cigar box. "Let's have a smoke, shall we?"

McDowell took two cigars from his mahogany humidor, clipped them both, and handed one to Henry. Once both were lit, he sat back down. "How are things in Richmond?" He asked.

Henry exhaled, seemingly quite satisfied with the quality of the cigar provided by the General, and responded, "General, President Davis has his cabinet in place, and the Generals are training our troops as best as possible. We are short of funds, equipment, uniforms, guns, and ammunition; you name it. My father, as you may be aware, is trying to enlist support from across the Atlantic as well as to our south. No one is necessarily jumping on the opportunity to come to our aid, not overtly, at least." (Long after the dust had settled from the Civil War, historians generally blamed Christopher Memminger for being unsuccessful in his efforts to maintain sufficient credit for the seceding states, thus leading to a perpetual struggle to find enough cash to fund the war effort. When one looks back, it is not hard to see why being Secretary of the Treasury for the rebel states would have been a very tall order for anyone.)

Henry continued, "With that being said, the spirit is high. The cause is just. If wars are won on the basis of who has the most passion, well, I would say we have the upper hand. Alas, my study of history at university was not that long ago, and I know that is not how wars are won. It takes money, arms, supplies, and the endless ability to deliver the same to the front lines. We are nowhere near ready on those fronts, Sir."

McDowell shifted his legs again and looked at Henry in such a way that made it clear he wanted him to continue. So he did. "We desperately need time, but it appears by all accounts that Mr. Lincoln has no patience for our plans." They both chuckled. "We are informed, Sir, that you intend to leave the capital and approach our troops in Virginia. We are rather hoping you can plan events to unfold in ways beneficial to our cause."

"Ah, there's the rub." McDowell finally spoke. "You would like to know our plans so you can strategize accordingly. Brilliant. I love it. Yes, I think we can work together, and you can skedaddle back to Richmond with the information you need. Does that work for you?"

Henry grinned and replied, "Yes, Sir, that will be just fine."

McDowell stood and went over to his desk. He picked up a manila folder and returned to the couch. He pulled a map out of the folder and unfolded it on the coffee table. Henry saw the label in the upper left corner of the map. It was handwritten, reading "Manassas Railroad Junction."

CHAPTER FOUR
HOW DID IT HAPPEN?

Richmond, Virginia,
July 10, 1861

Henry Memminger was shown in the rebel cabinet meeting room. Jeff Davis stood and pointed at an empty chair. "Good to see you, Henry. We have been waitin' on your report."

Henry sat down and nodded hello to all present and gave his dad a smile, "Hello, father."

Secretary of War Walker chimed in, "What do you have for us, son?" Leroy Pope Walker hailed from Alabama and was well-liked. Interestingly, he did not have a military background and would not actually last very long in his present position. He was there now, though.

"Mr. President, gentlemen, well, yes, I do have some information to impart, and I think it should set us up well for the confrontation to come."

Henry leaned forward and launched into an outline of his gathered intelligence. He noticed that Generals Johnston and Beauregard were present and was greatly relieved to see them in the room.

"The union army will move in 10 days, and the target is the Manassas railroad junction. They know that it is a key supply location for us, and they also know we have a concentration of troops in the area. It is the logical focal point for their first major campaign. McDowell will use Colonels Hunter and Heintzelman to move their divisions across Bull Run Creek to move from east to west. Generals Sherman and Porter will cover the west flank. Their aim is to pinch us near the Warrenton Turnpike and squeeze us right then and there. Except that it actually isn't the real goal." Memminger, the younger, paused.

Jeff Davis spoke, "OK, son, you have our attention. This is fascinating. How on earth have you gleaned this intelligence, and what exactly do you mean when you say that these are their plans but not actually?"

Henry took a deep breath and responded, "Well, Sir, you remember when I was last here, you briefed me on the fact that General McDowell was a friend of the cause?" Davis nodded affirmatively. "I decided to go to the source. So, I appropriated a union officer's uniform and gained entrance to his residence under false pretenses. Once in, I took the biggest gamble of my life and identified myself. Fortunately, my gamble worked, and for the next two hours, the General and I worked on a plan to ensure our victory."

"Damn boy, ya got a pair of balls on ya, I'll say that!" uttered Secretary of State Toombs. Everyone in the room laughed.

"Well, pray tell," Toombs continued, "What cockamamie plan you and the General concocted?"

Henry asked for a piece of paper and pencil, which were quickly provided. He drew a rough map of the Manassas area, pointing out Bull Run Creek running roughly north to south along the eastern edge and the Warrenton Turnpike running east to west on the northern side.

"Gentlemen," Henry continued, "General McClellan will approach from north of the Turnpike from what is known as Matthews Hill. He suggests you just send enough troops to meet his advancing line to be credible. Make the yanks think Matthews Hill is the battle line. But then, beat a disorderly retreat to make them think we're whupped. Then regroup on Henry Hill south of the Turnpike and pinch them when they chase us."

Jeff Davis spoke up. "So he will set the trap, and all we need to do is retreat and then smoke em!"

"Yes, Sir, that his how he plans to proceed, so it is now up to you, Generals." Henry looked up at Generals Beauregard and Johnston. "I should add that he is first going to send Commander Tyler to test out General Longstreet a few miles east of Manassas. We need to make sure Longstreet pours on the pressure, so Tyler will withdraw and move his forces over to join the army corps closer to Manassas. They will try to flank us from the west, so we just need to be ready for that once we retreat to Henry Hill."

General Johnston spoke up. "My boys are way too far west of where they need to be. They are in the Shenandoah. I will pull them back to the southeast and congregate them near the Junction."

Everyone nodded in agreement. "General Beauregard, it would appear your troops on Bull Run are right where they need to be."

Again, everyone nodded in agreement.

The stage was set. All the secessionists needed to do was follow the plan.

The White House, July 15, 1861

Things were finally progressing. It was Monday evening. The President knew that by no later than Sunday, his Generals would finally be seeking out the rebel forces in Virginia and engaging them. In a brief meeting that afternoon, General McDowell had attempted to delay the foray south into the next week by arguing that no good Christian should fight on a Sunday. Abe Lincoln had almost blown his top. But he had refrained and merely chided the General by saying, "Now, General, I first wanted to commend you for your victory at Rich Mountain four days ago. Not big, but a victory is a victory." (McClellan's troops had fended off a small rebel force and taken prisoners four days before.) What we are talking about here is a whole different kettle of fish. It is, one might say, a game-changer. I have the utmost confidence in our God above and in his infinite wisdom. If for some reason, he decides we should not fight on Sunday, I trust He will let us know. Why don't we proceed on the basis that He thinks it's a grand decision, shall we?" The General beat his retreat (something to which he would soon become quite accustomed). While anxious about the upcoming conflagration, Abe had nonetheless agreed to a small dinner in the living quarters on the 2nd Floor of the White House. He had not paid much attention to who was coming until just about now, 6 PM. He and Mary were both changing in their respective dressing areas. "Mary," he called to the next room. "With whom do we have the pleasure of dining tonight?"

"Oh Abe, I invited Salmon Chase and his daughter Kate. And also Mr. Nicolay. You work that boy too hard. He needs a girlfriend, and Miss Chase is certainly an eligible young lady about town."

There was no response for a few seconds. "Abe, are you there?"

"Oh yes," he replied, "that sounds wonderful." The President replayed her words and thought to himself, "John would be a lucky man to land Kate Chase."

"And the big surprise is that Elizabeth and Nin are here," her voice carried loudly into his dressing room. Elizabeth was Mary's older sister and one of the few calming influences in her life. In later years, after that horrid night at Ford's Theater, Robert Lincoln (Abe and Mary's oldest son) would actually commit her to an insane asylum. Elizabeth took Robert to court and had her released. No family exists without the good, the bad, and the ugly. Nin was Ninian Wirt Edwards, Elizabeth's husband; by all accounts, a stand-up fellow.

"They have come all the way from Springfield?" Abe inquired. The two couples had spent much time together in the two decades leading up to Lincoln's election.

"Why? Yes, dear, I thought I told you they were coming to visit us. They will be here for a week and are so looking forward to seeing the White House and watching you run our country!" Mary popped around the corner as she was finishing her sentence. She was wearing a pretty dress. Abe looked at her, and the thought occurred to him that the fabric looked awfully much like that which was on the chairs that had just been delivered to the living room. He pondered asking and then decided to himself, "What the hell!"

"Say, Mary, did Miss Keckley make that dress? That fabric looks very familiar." Elizabeth Keckley was a former slave who was now Mary Todd's dressmaker.

"Abe, you are so observant. She was with me a few weeks ago, and we were overseeing the delivery of some of our brand-new furniture. She had known that a large bolt had gone out and that a considerable amount of fabric was returned with the chairs in our living room. And she just snatched up that left-over bolt and said, 'Mrs. Lincoln, I'm a-gonna make you a dress with dis.' And she did! Isn't she wonderful? Isn't this dress magnificent?"

"It truly is, Mary, it truly is." The President replied. "No alcohol tonight for me, Mary. This is a nice quiet dinner, and I don't have to pretend I like alcohol for the gratification of our guests." The President had never really drunk much. He just didn't like the way it made him feel.

Mary had arranged dinner so that Abe sat at the head of the table on one end. Mary sat along the side so as to not make the odd number of dinner guesses throw off the symmetry of the seating plan. The dining table in the living quarters was no great monstrosity. It was mahogany, yet simple in its elegance, and could seat up to 10 people comfortably. On the President's left was Secretary Chase, and on his right was Kate. Next to Kate sat John Nicolay, and on his right was Nin Edwards. Sitting next to Secretary Chase was Mary's sister, Elizabeth, and Mary sat next to her and across from Nin.

Dinner was homespun, the way the Lincolns preferred. There was roast beef, mashed potatoes, and peas picked from a garden on the White House grounds. The White House had a small amount of French Bordeaux on hand, both red and white. A bottle of each was served and true to his word. The President drank only water.

Mary worked hard to get Kate and John to talk to one another while the President watched with seemingly detached amusement.

As dinner wound down over an apple pie, Abe mused, "I saw an article in Greeley's paper the other day. It said something along the lines of 'Celebrating the 4th of July should become American as apple pie'. I surely like that idea, and I hope it becomes true." Those around the table nodded in agreement. "I can tell they had a big firework show in Boston last week. That is a great way to have the people let off a little steam. Lord knows, with all this mess brewing, people need a distraction. I like that 'American as apple pie' line. I am going to start using it!" Everyone laughed.

There are some who argue the expression "as American as apple pie" originated in the late 1920s. Herbert Hoover's wife was apparently quite the cook and made a mean pie. Alas, that is just conjecture because whoever has been doing all the conjecturing clearly was not at the dinner table with Abe Lincoln on this particular warm night in July!

Nin changed the subject and brought up the more pressing matter of the moment. "So Abe," he began, "One couldn't help but notice in the carriage ride from Union Station to the White House there are an awful lot of soldiers milling about. Are we about to see some progress?"

"Indeed, Nin. Indeed", Abe responded. "I have been pushing and pushing. First General Scott, now General McDowell. And then there is General McClellan whispering in my ear. He thinks he is much better equipped to lead our army. We haven't even fought our first

60

battle of any consequence, and they are all jockeying for position. And let me tell you, I can read that McClellan like a book. That popinjay wants my job. He wants military victories so he can run as a democrat and occupy this seat right here!" The President pointed at his own chair.

"But I digress," he chuckled to himself. "Yes, I suspect we shall move toward the rebel forces in Virginia within the week. I am mighty concerned. Listening to the scuttlebutt around town, one would think this is going to be some kind of picnic. What a ridiculous sentiment. I pray to God our Generals are not leading complacent lambs to the slaughter. There is too much at stake."

Lincoln furrowed his brow, accentuating all those worry lines. "I apologize. We have had a nice dinner, and here I am ruining it."

"Not to worry, Abe," said Nin. "So tell us, what is old Fuss and Feathers doing? Is he organizing things? We seem to read nothing about him. (Fuss and Feathers was a nickname General Scott had earned somewhere along the way in his career. It emanated from his being a stickler for military procedure and dress)

"Humph," grunted the President. "He is our titular leader. He does have a plan of sorts. He calls it the Anaconda plan. He wants us to own the Mississippi and then push east and strangle the enemy. Looks good on paper. Sounds good. But for heaven's sake, I can't even get our Generals to leave this city!"

That same evening, some 100 miles to the south of the White House, Jeff Davis was having dinner in his Richmond townhouse with Generals Beauregard and Johnston. General Johnston was his senior officer and, ironically, had the distinction of having been the most senior officer in the United States Army to have defected to the southern cause.

Jeff Davis did not enjoy the opulence of the White House, but what he lacked in size and grandeur he made up for with high-quality food, wine, and service. For now, at least, the rebels did not want for extravagances. Over the ensuing four years, all that would change.

Davis clicked his fingers, and a negro servant appeared. "More wine, boy." He said dismissively. "Yes, Suh," replied the young man, who was dressed to the nines. As the wine was poured, Davis spoke, "Generals, are we ready? I must say I am relishing the fact that we are planning a mini-anaconda move. General Scott would be proud of us. When all this mess is behind us, I surely hope to be able to celebrate with him and General McDowell. So, are we ready?"

General Johnston responded. "Mr. President, as you will recall from our previous conversation, General Beauregard's troops are right where they need to be. Mine are on the way back east from the Shenandoah. They will be in place by the 21st. If young Memminger is correct, we will be ready for the enemy's approach that day."

Jeff Davis looked at General Beauregard. "This isn't going to be the picnic Fort Sumpter was, you know." It was a statement, not a question. (Little did President Davis appreciate the irony of this comment. But more on that later.)

"Yes, Mr. President, I'm fully aware that Fort Sumpter will go down as the easiest feather in my cap. I am under no illusions that, notwithstanding our superior information and planning capability resulting therefrom, men will die, and it will be a fight. I take comfort that we have men like Jackson, Longstreet, and others by our sides. They are leaders. Their men will follow them anywhere. I don't think that spirit exists up north."

He continued, "I have briefed them all. They know the plan. Attack, stand firm, waver, and retreat, so the main blue corps charges Henry Hill. Between us on the east and General Johnston's troops to the south and west, we will tidy things up." General Johnston nodded affirmatively. Jeff Davis just smiled and motioned for another very fine glass of claret.

Washington, D.C., July 16, 1861

The morning following his dinner in the White House, Abe Lincoln stood on Pennsylvania Avenue and watched thousands of troops and copious amounts of supplies begin to stream south out of the city. Manassas Junction was 30 miles to the southwest of the nation's capital. Someone swift afoot could probably make the walk-in twelve to thirteen hours. These Yankee troops were anything but swift afoot! General McDowell figured they would cover, on average, 8 to 10 miles a day, taking into consideration the numbers of men, rations, weapons, and ammunition. He wasn't wrong. The troops were finally on location by July 20th.

CHAPTER FIVE
THE CULMINATION

Manassas Junction,
July 20, 1861

On the afternoon of the day, they arrived; Generals McDowell, Hunter, Burnside, and Tyler surveyed the topography to their south. They stood on Matthews Hill, the place from which they had planned to launch their assault. The enemy camps were dotting the landscape in front of them. It all seemed surreal.

General McDowell looked over his left shoulder to the east toward the Bull Run Stream. There was a stone bridge his troops had secured, but a little further north from there and slightly behind his lines. He did a double-take and muttered, "Please tell me I am not seeing what I think I am seeing." The other generals turned to look, and all four of their faces reflected a mixture of anxiety, incredulity, and shock. There in the distance, well within what anyone would consider a circumference of hostile potential, came dozens of horse-drawn wagons, most of them downright "citified." These were not country folk.

"Will one of you tell me what in tarnation is happening?" No one spoke a single word. Rather, General Hunter spurred his horse and rode off toward the caravan of approaching carriages. As Hunter approached them, he was stunned to recognize a couple congressmen, their wives, and many from Washington's well-to-do socialite set. He pulled alongside the lead wagon and spoke, "Hello, folks. I am General Hunter." They nodded and smiled back at him. "You appear to be crossing the ford here and approaching what may be a battleground as soon as tomorrow. May I ask what you are doing?"

A pompous man in a three-piece suit with a bowler hat sitting inside the carriage, holding a glass of champagne, responded, "Why, General? We have been waiting for this day for months. We've packed vittles and supplies enough to last us all the way to Richmond! We want to see the rebs capitulate. We want to be there for it. It should be a jolly good show!"

Hunter was beside himself. He raised his voice so as many people could hear him as possible. "Ladies and Gentlemen. I cannot make you leave. But I must tell you this journey upon which you have embarked is ill-advised. Anything can happen. There is no such thing as a cakewalk to Richmond. I strongly urge you to return home."

The General stopped and noted that the progression of carriages was once again proceeding toward the Yankee encampment. He shook his head, pulled on his reigns, and began to turn his horse around. "General," came a female voice from one of the oncoming carriages, "We have sandwiches and petit fours. Why don't you join us?"

"Very kind, ma'am. I must take a raincheck." He then spoke loudly again. "And I strongly urge the lot of you to re-cross the creek. You are in danger here." With that, the General rode back to his fellow generals.

"General?" McDowell looked inquisitively at Hunter.

"Sir, they have come to watch the show. They brought picnics. They think they will tag along with us to Richmond."

"Jesus Christ!" exclaimed McDowell. "Sorry, gentlemen, I do not usually swear. But that is the most stupid thing I have ever heard. Is this some cocktail party circuit idea? Who is dumb enough to think this is smart? Did you tell them to leave?"

"I did, Sir. But I am not sure if they took me seriously."

If Jeff Davis could have been a fly on the wall, he would have recalled his recent statement that the upcoming battle would not be any picnic. He would no doubt chuckle as it appeared that is exactly what some people thought was about to happen.

The Yankee generals discussed rations and the importance of feeding the troops well that night; protein and carbs. Even in the middle of the nineteenth century, they knew they didn't want soldiers going into battle on an empty stomach. General McDowell asked about the positioning of the cannon, and when satisfied, he bid them adieu, with the final reminder that he expected a charge toward rebel lines at 8 AM the following morning.

Rebel Camp, near Henry Hill, July 20ʹ 1861- Evening

Thomas Jackson was not well known amongst the rebel rank and file. He had fought in the Mexican War but had retired years before the outbreak of hostilities in this conflagration. He had been teaching at the Virginia Military Institute in Lexington. Jackson was taciturn, sober, and tough. Any number of his ex-students would attest to those attributes. General Johnston plucked him out of obscurity and brought him into his inner circle of leaders.

Unlike Jackson, Pete Longstreet had remained in the US Army for 20 years after his graduation from West Point. He had served admirably, but as with so many of his West Point mates, he chose his state over the union and fought for Jeff Davis. He was assigned to General Beauregard and had already distinguished himself at Blackburn's Ford two days earlier (McDowell's advancing lines had tried to cross the Ford and were repelled. What is lost in history is whether the southern victory was real or McDowell simply wanted to keep his troops together until the decisive rout he was planning for the 21ˢᵗ).

On this evening of July 20, it was hot. The troops (both blue and grey) had long since shed their woolen jackets. They were stripped

66

down to their pants, shirt, and ammo kits. The officers were no exception.

Longstreet had graduated from West Point in 1842, four years earlier than Thomas Jackson. Of the two, Jackson distinguished himself far more in the classroom, which perhaps explains why he ended up teaching. One thing we have all learned in the study of warfare and leaders is that classroom performance is no guarantee of success in life, politics, or the battlefield. Longstreet fell into the category of those who underachieved in the classroom but excelled in the real world. Ironically, another such General who fell into that category was Ulysses Grant; more on that later.

The two men sat close to their fire but not too close. They certainly did not need the warmth it was generating. It was about 84 degrees as the time approached 9 PM, just dark, and the fireflies were out. There were trees, but most of the land had been cleared over the past one hundred and fifty years. Around them was rolling farmland. The grass had already been trampled by the men, horses, and wagons. It was mostly brown, as the lush green spring grass had given way to the sultry heat of a Virginia summer.

Longstreet spoke, "So Beauregard has us engaging and falling back. I'm still not quite sure why. Are you?"

Jackson picked up a stick and cleared some space in the dirt near the fire. "Lookee here," he said. "The way I see it, we're just gonna play with these yanks for a bit and fall back to form a U around them as they advance against our retreat. It's been done before. Wellington at Waterloo…worked like a charm. Anyway, I'm jes waiting for General Johnston to catch up and cover our western flank. I can't quite explain how my regiment is the only one sittin' around twiddlin' its thumbs."

"Well, thank you for the history lesson about Waterloo, professor!" Longstreet laughed. "I imagin' yer here 'cause yer such a hardass, and you drove yer men faster than anyone else. Then again, they follow you, so that is what matters." Both men nodded. "What I can't figure out is why old Irvin will willingly have his troops run after us? Would you?"

"Hell no, I wouldn't!" exclaimed Jackson. "But then again, all we hear is how old Abe wants them to fight and march on Richmond. They know Jeff Davis is convening the confederate Congress today. Given their druthers, they would rather stop those boys from makin' their plans. Well, those fellas over yonder on Matthews and Buck Hills have no idea what is about to hit 'em, do they now? I reckon Beauregard and Johnston are just countin' on them being too eager. I guess we're fixin' to find out tomorrow."

Longstreet stretched his legs out. "Yep, I reckon so." He paused, and while he did, both men stared into the fire, thinking about things far away. "I miss Maria," he said somewhat wistfully (Longstreet had married the daughter of a US general more than a decade before, and the two would ultimately have ten children, not all of whom survived childhood).

"And I miss my Mary Anna," Jackson responded. Jackson had married before, but his first wife lost her life during childbirth. He married Mary Anna in 1857, just four short years ago, when he was settled in academic life in Lexington. Things had certainly changed for both these men. Little did they know that they both would become some of the most trusted, successful southern commanders.

Both men didn't feel the need to say much more. Jackson was catching and releasing fireflies. Longstreet kept staring into the fire. Eventually, he stood up. "Well, Thomas, let's go out there and do our jobs tomorrow. I know you will, and I certainly hope to hold up my end of the bargain."

Jackson looked at him and said, "Of course, you will, my friend. Contrary to what those people over a mile yonder up that hill may think," He pointed toward the Yankee lines, "it isn't gonna be any picnic, but we will prevail, no doubt." Truer words were never spoken.

Generals James Longstreet and Thomas "Stonewall" Jackson at Manassas

Manassas Junction, July 21, 1861

The Yankee shelling from the Bull Run area began a little past daylight. The noise was thunderous. To the rebel soldiers on the receiving end, the barrage seemed endless. Most of the troops had dug in and were protected from the cannon fire and grapeshot contained in many of the fired shots. Grapeshot was murderous. It ripped bodies apart. It was designed to mutilate humans, and it was effective.

The idea was to soften the rebel lines. It certainly was not a novel strategy. The tactic had been used since the advent of gunpowder. After the shelling, the Yankee troops advanced and were met by the opposition. The fighting was intense, and casualties mounted on both sides. But after a couple of hours of fighting, as planned, the union troops surged and pushed the grey coats back to Henry Hill. Amazingly, the picnic brigade lined up in their carriages across Bull Run Creek and began to applaud. It was quite a show, and their boys appeared to be winning. They were just far enough to be away from the blood and guts.

McDowell had laid the trap for his own army. Fighting was intense through the early afternoon. Then Beauregard and Johnston sent their reinforcements in from the rear, east, and west of Henry Hill. Prospects for a northern victory were dimming quickly. There was a moment around 4 PM when confederate General Barnard Bee (who would die a short time later) rallied his troops to counter-attack by pointing up the Hill to Thomas Jackson. "Look at that, fellas! General Jackson is standing there like a stone wall!" Indeed, Jackson was in the middle of his troops, unflinching and encouraging them to turn the blue tide away. From that moment on, he became known as Stonewall Jackson.

It was at that time that the trademark rebel was created. When the counter-charge began, leaders like Stonewall Jackson urged them on. These farm boys from the south screamed, hooted, and hollered at the top of their lungs as they charged toward their retreating enemy. From that moment on, the battle was, for all intents and purposes, over. The northern army was pinched and began to take flight. Within the space of twenty minutes, the battlefield was chaos as thousands of northern army soldiers turned tail and ran back to where they had started hours ago. And they didn't stop.

The socialites and politicians were astounded to see a blue wave of petrified battle-weary men streaming toward and past them. One young lieutenant ran past them screaming, "They're hobgoblins, I'll tell you. Run before it is too late!"

It was then the revelers realized they would soon be swamped by rebel troops. They began to beat a disorderly and hasty retreat. Picnic baskets were left on their blankets. Chairs sat in place with no one left to occupy them. Once the route was complete and the union forces were miles away, beating their path back toward Washington, several rebel troops sat down on those blankets and enjoyed some very good food and champagne. It was a fitting end to a brutal but very successful day for the southern army.

The unanswered question for the Confederates was why they did not keep chasing the northern army. It was almost as though they had planned the route but forgotten to contemplate how they should capitalize on a fleeing Yankee army. Until this day, historians have struggled to rationalize this mistake. But hindsight is always 20-20.

The White House, July 25, 1861

Abe Lincoln stared at Irvin McDowell, General Winifred Scott, and the Secretary of War Simon Cameron. They were in a meeting downstairs in the Green Room, a ceremonial meeting room that had been used as anything from Jefferson's dining room to Monroe's card room. It was adjacent to the formal East Room and was now used more or less for ceremonial meetings. But that was not why the President had come downstairs for today's meeting. They sat there now because General Scott could not make it up the circular staircase leading to Lincoln's office and living quarters.

"General," Lincoln began, "Thank you for coming over to see me. I am sure this is not an easy meeting."

The General sat up and crossed his legs. "No, Sir, Mr. President. I certainly understand your desire to meet and be briefed on the events

71

earlier this week. I am aware, Sir, that things did not turn out as we planned."

Lincoln and Cameron looked at him incredulously. Cameron spoke. "General, you had months to prepare our troops. You outnumbered the enemy. You had better arms, munitions, and equipment. Sir, how on earth did this happen?"

McDowell feigned hurt. "Secretary Cameron, warfare is unpredictable. We had no idea they would reinforce their side so stoutly. We didn't see it coming."

Lincoln cleared his throat. "General, I am relieving you of your command. General Scott, I request that you find General McClellan and ask him to come to the White House. I will be asking him to form a new Army of the Potomac. One that is ready to fight and to win."

Irvin McDowell looked crestfallen and ensured the President he would continue to faithfully serve his country in whatever capacity was requested of him. He hadn't seen it coming. He took his leave and would never again visit the White House.

General Scott looked at both Lincoln and Cameron. As he stared across the Green Room at them, he mused that little did either of them know ole Fuss and Feathers had begun the long, drawn-out strategy that had just recently resulted in the very embarrassing Yankee loss at Manassas Junction. McDowell was out, but here he sat, imposingly; well, in a manner of speaking, at least. "I believe General McClellan is en route to Washington via train, gentlemen. He should be here by the morning, and I shall ride over to the place to gather him and return. He will no doubt be very pleased to learn of this promotion."

"Of that, I have no doubt," said the President. "He is an ambitious man, and like so many of my cabinet officers," the President paused and looked at Secretary Cameron, "I'm sure he would love to be sitting in my chair in four years. Hah, by that time, I reckon I might be ready to let the dog catcher have it!"

Secretary Cameron cleared his throat and said, "Rest assured, Mr. President, while I may have harbored some ambitions to reach the high office you have attained, from what I have seen during these last few months, you can have it!" All three men laughed. Cameron looked at the spoon he had been using to help dissolve the sugar in his teacup. He held it up. "TJ is the scripted initials on it. I wonder if President Jefferson left some of his silver behind."

Lincoln responded, "I wouldn't doubt that for a second. First, the White House was sparsely outfitted sixty years ago, and of course, they had to start all over again when the British came back in 1812 for another crack at us. You would have thought they had learned their lesson. I suppose they went home knowing that at least they burned the President's house down. I heard Dolly Madison put some people to work and saved whatever art, china, and whatever else they could carry before the torches did their work. I'll bet my bottom dollar she saved that silver spoon you are using, and it was left behind by Jefferson." He paused and then continued. "What an amazing republic! That all seems so long ago, and yet it was only, what, fourscore and five years ago that those great men declared independence? We have citizens still alive who were born before July 4, 1776. It has been less than a century. Remarkable, isn't it? And here I sit doing the job done by Washington, Adams, and Jefferson. Anything is possible in this great country. Of course, if you read Mr. Greely's paper, you would think my election heralded the re-emergence of the dark ages! Well, I certainly hope we all can prove him wrong on that front. Good heavens, the fate of our union depends on our success."

"Hear, hear," said General Scott, as he slowly and painfully lifted himself up from his chair. The gout was now almost always a debilitating part of his day-to-day life. He hobbled toward the door to the main corridor where his driver awaited him. Turning around and standing in the door frame, he said, "I shall see you tomorrow, as soon as I have collected the General."

With just the two of them left, the President looked at Cameron. "Simon, how is it that I have been left with a choice between twiddle dee or twiddle dum? Why have our best soldiers chosen to fight for the Confederacy?"

Cameron took a moment or two to decide whether the President really wanted an answer and decided he did. "Well, Sir, I cannot explain things as fully as either of us would like, but I can tell you that in my studies of our short military history, West Point has been turning out more qualified southern officers for the past fifty years. They just seem to be hungrier and, dare I say, smarter?" Lincoln looked skeptical. "I know, that sounds irrational. But look at our best fighters before this unpleasantness began. They are nearly all from southern states. Maybe our northern industrial states have become more complacent. We have the financial markets. We have an industrial base. I don't know. I am grasping at straws."

"It's as good answer as any, Simon. But it still doesn't help me with what we are going to do to light a fire under twiddle-dum when he walks into this meeting. Manassas has ended along with any false hopes or delusions about an easy victory. This war is bad. It's damned bad."

Old Fuss and Feathers-Winfield Scott

Richmond, Virginia,
July 25, 1861

The Confederate Congress was in its fifth day of the session. In addition to the business of running a new nation, the gathered delegates took time out to give a rousing standing ovation to Generals Johnston and Beauregard. One would have thought they had won the war. But all things considered, it was quite understandable that these two men were received warmly.

Although unplanned, General Johnston spoke briefly. Using his arms to motion quiet and ask the attendees to sit, Johnston said, "I am not a public speaker. I am a fighter." Before he could get another word in, the hall erupted again, and there was another standing ovation.

General Beauregard stood by his side, smiling, and whispered, "I don't think you'll have to say all that much!"

Johnston continued, "I know there are already some who criticize our decision not to chase the Yankees back to, hell, back to New York City!" Again, the room erupted, and the applause and yelling lasted another two minutes. Johnston finally raised his arms again and implored the group to sit. "But gentlemen, General Beauregard and I have spent our adult lives studying warfare. One thing we know for sure is that only a fool proceeds without a plan. We had a plan at Manassas. Our plan did not take us beyond that ground. There are far too many variables, too many things that could have gone pear-shaped had we strayed from the plan. We did what we set out to do and marked my words; we will do it again!" The delegates rose again and began stomping their feet. Unseen at this time was President Davis, who had come in through a side door and was witnessing the spectacle. He smiled.

Johnston raised his voice and came to a conclusion. "We have a cause. We want the right to run our states without being told what to do by another power. Even a power right here in what used to be the United States. They may have more money. They may have more men. They may have more guns. Yes, that is all true. But they don't have what we have. Gentlemen, we possess the will to win!" Before they could interrupt him again, he finished, "We will not stop. We will not be discouraged. They take their freedom for granted. We do not. We will fight until we are free. Our cause is just. With God on our side, we shall prevail. Thank you. God Bless you, and God Bless these Confederate States of America!"

The two Generals turned toward the door and were then greeted by Jeff Davis, who embraced them warmly. "Well done, General." He laughed, "For a man who doesn't relish public speaking, you certainly know how to get a crowd riled up."

The racket was very loud, and both Generals heaved sighs of relief when they shut the door behind them and found themselves on a quiet Richmond Street. Beauregard said, "Well, that was the easy part. Now we have to figure out how to actually win."

"I know, Pierre, I know. Riling up a bunch of old politicians is a hella lot easier than actually winning a war." The two of them ambled down the street, kicking ideas around and formulating plans for a way forward. They realized before they parted company that they would have to sit down with Jeff Davis and talk strategy.

The White House, July 26, 1861

Secretary Cameron, John Nicolay, and the President were in the Green Room. Lincoln had asked Nicolay to join him and Cameron while waiting for General McClellan to arrive with General Scott. They had talked about all sorts of matters in the nearly two hours they spent waiting on their arrival. The President had begun to appreciate Nicolay's "younger" outlook on the pressing matters of the day. He did not take lightly the fact that Nicolay considered the defeat at Manassas to be an ominous sign that the war was likely to be a long, drawn-out affair.

They heard the two Generals approaching the Green Room. Lincoln stood up in anticipation of their entrance. Nicolay and Cameron followed suit, and Cameron moved over to a chair closer to Lincoln's, thus making his seat available to General Scott. Its design offered easier ingress and egress.

General McClellan strutted into the room ahead of the slower General Scott. Lincoln took a quick glance behind him to see if any peacock feathers were following. There was an awkward moment as he turned around in anticipation of Scott, but all anyone heard was labored breathing making its way down the hall. After a ten-second pregnant pause, Scott's figure consumed the doorway.

"Ah, there you are," said Lincoln. "Welcome back, and welcome to you, George. Please, why don't you both have a seat?"

General Scott found the right chair. Nicolay started to leave, but Lincoln motioned him to stay. "So, General McClellan, I suspect you have been briefed and know why you are here?"

"Yes, sir, Mr. President. I am here to gratefully accept your request that I form up a new Army of the Potomac. I am, Sir, however, as immodest as it may seem, the right man for the job. Sometimes out of adversity comes opportunity. And I feel this defeat at Manassas will be looked back upon in such a light."

Lincoln looked warily at him and said, "Well, General, we all hope you are right. The fate of the Union depends on it. I know you have had some success in the west over the past couple of months. I know Mr. Chase is a big supporter of yours. What I don't know is whether these positives are enough to make you the right choice to assemble this army of ours and take over the rebels; win this thing once and for all." He paused. General McClellan said nothing. He just stared at the President, which Lincoln found very annoying. "General Scott assures me you are up to the task. Are you?"

McClellan cleared his throat. "Mr. President, I have never taken on a task I could not complete and complete with unquestioned success. It is simply who I am." He looked down at his navy tunic, replete with brass buttons and medals, and saw what looked like a foggy spot on one of his buttons. Grabbing a handkerchief from his pocket, he rubbed the button until it glistened. This all happened in the space of a few seconds. Then he looked up at the President as if to enquire whether more of response was required.

"Your confidence is applaudable, General," said Secretary Cameron. "I know this is all-new at the moment, but the President and I would be appreciative if you could share any initial thoughts you may have."

McClellan sat upright in his chair and cleared his throat. "Well, begging your pardons, sirs, but I must say the pressure to engage the enemy was one of the reasons we lost at Manassas. Our troops are unpolished. They have no idea how to perform under fire. We must slow down the pace and train our forces. And of course, Mr. President, there is the transition to manage. I can hardly just walk into this new role without preparations being made." He adjusted his starched blue tunic and made sure the buttons were straight. "After all, I will not even have new stationery with my title until August 20. If for no other reason, I think that is the day I should officially assume this new job."

Lincoln slouched in his chair and held his head in his two hands. "Good Lord, General, I feel like I am on some sort of wheel that keeps turning round and round but is stuck in the mud, making absolutely no progress. We have trained these boys for months! It's not about stationery, for Pete's sake!"

"Well, Sir, yes, but who is Pete?"

"It is an expression, General; one concocted for those who prefer not to swear. If you would prefer, I will say things more bluntly. Let's get this moving, for Christ's sake!"

"Oh, I see. Well, whatever, but Sir, I haven't been responsible for the training. I need time. Things will be different. You shall see."

Lincoln's eyes bored into McClellan, "I will be patient, General, but not interminably. You have a window. Please use it. I would prefer that our relationship be one based on shared goals and shared successes."

The meeting drew to a close shortly thereafter, and all but Nicolay had departed.

"What have I wrought, John? Why does this have to be so painfully difficult?"

Nicolay looked at him. "Sir, I wish I had an answer. I truly do. From my perspective, all I can say is I wish we could switch generals with Jeff Davis. It seems he got the best of them."

Lincoln grunted in agreement. "Well, onward and upwards. Let's see if McClellan gets on his horse and moves with dispatch. Was he winding me up about the stationery? Could he possibly have been serious?"

Nicolay shrugged, "I did not sense irony, Mr. President." Lincoln just shook his head.

As he left the room, Nicolay could tell Lincoln was not going to have a good day.

The Popinjay-George B. McClellan

CHAPTER SIX
THE LULL

Richmond, Virginia,
August 2, 1861

Henry Memminger finally had a moment to catch his breath. In the last several months, he had played a pivotal role in supplying the southern command with key information about the Yankee battle plan. August marked a lull in the storm. In retrospect and in the grander scheme of things, it was more like the eye of a hurricane. Things were calm, but all around him, events that were unfolding meant things would be stormy for years to come.

On this day, though, he finally had some time to spend with Janie Frank, a moment he had thought about for far too long. It was a hot, humid August day. Henry and Janie walked hand in hand down East Grace Street toward the oldest part of downtown Richmond. At 23rd Street, he asked her, "Whose house is that?" as he pointed at a stately house on the corner.

"Oh, that is Elizabeth Van Lew's house. She is quite an active socialite; she seems as though she knows everyone. She's a widow, I heard. I do not know her." She looked at him as she spoke. He gazed back at her as though she was the only person on the planet. If all of Richmond had been ablaze, Henry Memminger would not have noticed. He had read of such love and was sure he was one of the lucky few to know what it meant. His look was not lost on Janie. "Henry, why are you looking at me like a little puppy dog. I swear you look just like my Labrador puppy momma brought back from England."

The Frank family had visited England with some regularity. Notwithstanding his Virginia roots, Janie's father had a large plantation in South Carolina, which describes how the Memminger and Frank families had originally met. He sailed overseas to stay in touch with the commodity market traders in London city. It was the only way to ensure he could sell his cotton at top dollar. He always took his wife, Sarah, and Janie with him. Thomas Patrick Henry Frank was something of an anglophile and believed his wife and daughter would be better-rounded with occasional exposure to people on the other side of the pond. The Labrador breed would not actually be introduced in the United States until the early twentieth century, so it is possible Janie's puppy was the first lab to ever set foot on US soil.

"Henry, it is so nice to see you, and you know I do love being with you, but you make me nervous when you stare at me like that."

Henry put his head back and laughed. "Ok, then, I will stop. But it isn't easy, I'll tell you that much. I love everything about you. You know that, don't you?" He looked at her pleadingly. It was interesting that this young man, who had risked his life repeatedly over the past six months as he traveled back and forth from Richmond to Washington, felt absolutely powerless when he was with her.

"Oh, Henry," she stopped and turned to face him, taking both of his hands in hers, "Of course, I know that. And if you don't know that I am yours, forever, then you are a stupid boy!" She laughed. He laughed. Life was good. They continued their wonderful, carefree walk down East Grace Street.

About five blocks down the street, near 18th Street, Henry thought about Janie's comment several minutes before. "What did you say that lady's name is? Who owns that nice house back there?"

"Who?" She asked. "Oh, you mean Elizabeth Van Lew. Why?"

"That name is so familiar, but I can't for the life of me figure out why I should know her, or at least know of her." Henry kept walking, lost in thought, trying to put two and two together and come up with something that helped him to solve his question. He was not just perplexed. He was bothered. Something about that name made him nervous.

And then he stopped. He made the connection. Janie looked at him inquisitively. "Janie, I think she may be a spy. I have seen her in Washington. In fact, I have seen her with General McClellan. I need to find out if she is there on our behalf. I mean, I guess it's possible we could have several tentacles spreading out in the Capital, me being one of them, and I don't know all of them. That makes sense, I guess." His brow was furrowed. He was troubled, lost in the possibilities implicit in his answer having now connected the dots.

"If she is sympathetic to the Union, what does that mean?" She asked. "I mean, obviously, she will need to be incarcerated, but what does it mean for you?"

"If I know about her, then she may know about me. And if she knows about me, she will have told others, and then, Janie, it means my days in Washington are over. I am already on Nicolay's list, but if McClellan has his army actively looking for me, I am done. I will have to find another way to help our cause."

"Henry, don't fret over that now. Let's enjoy our day. You can find out easily enough when you next see President Davis."

She stopped and looked into his eyes. "Anyway, I would like you to kiss me."

He said, "Here, in public?"

"Yes, you fool. Go on. Break the rules!" She laughed. He laughed. Then, he kissed her. Life was good again, and Elizabeth Van Lew was momentarily forgotten.

Henry pitched up at Jeff Davis's office at 9 AM the following day. As he sat in the waiting foyer, he was told the President was not in but was expected shortly. The waiting room was comfortable and set the stage for Davis's office and meeting table. There was no shortage of English mahogany furniture. The floors were made of hardwood pine, with a slightly worn oriental rug covering about two-thirds of the floor space. Henry had previously noted that everything about this residence was much nicer than the furniture and décor he had seen in the White House. But he did acknowledge to himself that the White House was much bigger, and also, he never had the opportunity to see all the improvements Mary Todd Lincoln had made. He knew about them because they were covered with regularity in the Richmond Dispatch, the favored newspaper of the day. The editors followed Mrs. Lincoln's spending sprees with glee and regularly reported on her spendthrift ways.

Henry noticed that day's edition of the Dispatch on the coffee table and picked it up to read. The war, which was basically being waged via various skirmishes along the coast westward toward the Mississippi, dominated the pages of the paper. Henry noticed the one-cent price on the upper right-hand corner and thought to himself that he would willingly double the price he paid if that meant the paper would have fewer advertisements (without advertising, no newspapers could afford to go to print. For those who think your newspapers have too little news and too many ads, you would have been appalled at the amount of advertising in mid-nineteenth century publications).

There was an editorial about General McClellan's preparations for the Army of the Potomac. Amazingly, there had been very little news of developments in the week that had transpired since news of McClellan's appointment found its way to Richmond. McClellan was quoted in the article, and as Henry read the same, he muttered to himself, "Same old tripe. Nothing changes up there. Bully for us. They are all hell-bent on helping our cause."

The portion of the editorial that elicited this response was excerpted from the New York Tribune and said, "General McClellan took time away from his duties and told us 'I will not rest until we have accomplished our task. Naturally, though, we must be cautious. I will officially assume my duties on August 20. There is much transitional work to be performed. We are in no hurry. Theirs is the side that seceded. They must defeat us. Time is on our side. We will train. We will prepare. We will bide our time.' We, the editorial leadership, encourage Mr. Lincoln to light a proverbial fire under his General. Haven't we already seen this script played out at Manassas? Is there something in the water in Washington that cause delay and borderline prevarication? We hope not. Delay is not what this nation needs to see if we are to preserve the Union."

Henry mused that it was a good thing Horace Greeley wasn't running the Union military. He imagined that there would be further movement toward Richmond and other strategic positions than had so far been seen.

At that moment, Jeff Davis walked through the door and saw Henry reading the paper. "Well, there is a pleasant surprise." Henry stood up. Davis swept across the room, saying, "C'mon in, Henry."

Davis entered his office and then turned around to shake Henry's hand. "Let's sit over here by the fireplace." He motioned to a sitting area with the customary couch and two chairs placed around a brick fireplace. Davis sat on the couch, and Henry chose one of the chairs. "How are you, boy? You look fine enough." Before Henry could answer, Davis jumped up and went to his desk. "That reminds me of something. Is your father in town?"

Henry said, "I saw him last night, and he said he was coming over this morning to talk paper currency issues with you."

"Arrgghhh," said President Davis. "Money will be the bane of our existence if this mess gets too drawn out. The damn yanks control the means of production."

At that moment, there was a knock on the door, and Davis's servant popped his head in to say, "Secretary Memminger is here suh".

"Let him in, let him in", Davis said with a dismissive wave of the hand.

Christopher Memminger strode in, saw his son, smiled, and then walked over to shake his President's hand.

"Have a seat, Chris. I'm glad you are here. I have been waiting for young Henry to visit." Davis reached into his right-hand, top desk drawer and pulled out a black velvet box. It was about an inch thick and some eight inches top to bottom. President Davis opened it and pulled out a silver and bronze medal fashioned as a ten-point star. It bore the great seal of the Confederate states and under the seal were the words "Honor, Duty, Valor, and Devotion."

"Henry", Davis walked over to the younger Memminger and said, "In this conflagration, I suspect there will be times I have to make this award posthumously. Well, in truth, I am not sure I will ever award this medal again. My generals do not think it is appropriate to recognize individual valor. They believe we must sink or swim together. So this medal, to be honest, is a prototype that may never see the light of day. So, you are the very first recipient of the Confederate States' Medal of Honor. And you may be the very last! Congratulations, Son. You are a brave young man, whose service in the months leading up to the battle near Manassas Junction was critical to our success. I thank you. Your country thanks you." With those words, he placed the grey and yellow ribbon over Henry's head and let the medal rest on his chest (in point of fact, there actually was a medal such as the one described herein that ended up never being awarded because of aforementioned reason).

Henry's father had known the occasion was on the docket, but did not know the exact timing. As such, he was almost as surprised. He was certainly the more emotional of the two, as one would expect a good father to be. His eyes were moist as he went to his son, grabbed his hand, and shook it vigorously. "I am proud of you, son; damned proud. And to think when you were having such a good time up north at Harvard, I wasn't sure you would amount to a hill of beans!" All three of them laughed.

Davis let them enjoy the moment and then said, "Alright then. Chris, I know you are here to discuss our currency issues. Let's see what's on Henry's mind first. What brought you here this morning, son?"

All three of them sat down and Henry began. The rising sun from the east was streaming through the windows and casting an almost surreal light on Davis's face. The president was so focused on Henry, he seemed not to notice.

Henry began, "Sir, does the name Elizabeth Van Lew ring any bells?" Henry traded glances with his father and Davis. They both looked quizzically back at him. "You see, I was with Janie today, and, oh sorry, Sir." He looked at the President and went on to say, "Janie is a lady friend of mine. Anyway, we were on East Grace Street and I asked who owned a nice-looking house out on about 23rd Street. She told me it belongs to Elizabeth Van Lew. Well, nothing struck me at the time, except I had a lingering feeling about that name. Something was nagging on me. And a few minutes later, I realized I had seen and heard of that lady in Washington."

Jeff Davis's face showed that his interest was now piqued. "Go on", he said.

"It dawned on me that you could easily have several spies working on our behalf in Washington, and there is no particular reason I should know about any of them. But Sir, I thought I would check, because you see, I have actually seen her with General McClellan."

Davis's eyes narrowed. Henry had paused and was looking at him for some kind of response. "Henry, as usual, your instincts are spot on. So to be totally frank, yes, of course I have other people working on our behalf in and among the northern ranks. None, I might add, have been as productive as have you. And you are right, who they are is a need-to-know matter, but it is actually in your best interests that you don't know. Now that said, that woman is not one of them. We may have a problem on our hands. Chris do you know of her?"

Henry's father shifted in his chair and responded "I believe I do, Sir. Perhaps you and I can take this up before we discuss our monetary challenges?"

Henry took that as his cue, and left, knowing that he had done the right thing. He put his medal back in its case and, having been thanked again by President Davis, began walking to the Frank house to see his best friend Janie.

"Chris, you obviously have something to tell me about this woman. What is it?" said Davis.

"Jeff, I feel bad, and I detest being the one to reveal this, but I fear our Secretary Walker is in over his head." Leroy Pope Walker was the Confederate Secretary of War. He was from Huntsville, Alabama, as was his wife Eliza. Both of them would return after the war and die there a couple decades later.

"Pray tell, what does that mean?" said Davis.

"Well, I reckon he may be rather intimate with Miss Van Lew. And I do not believe that is something about which Eliza has any knowledge." Memminger paused after dropping that bombshell.

"Good Lord", Davis exclaimed, "You are telling me that our Secretary of War is covertly cavorting with a lady who has been seen in Washington with McClellan?"

"I'm afraid so, Sir. I wish it were not so. Leroy is a good man, Jeff. I do not doubt his loyalties. I may question his choice as Secretary of War, but that is neither here nor there, nor is it my business. I believe he has been quietly seeing her for the past few months. And based on Henry's intelligence, it could well be that she has insinuated herself into his life to extract information on our enemy's behalf."

Davis got up and started pacing back and forth across his office. "We need to get to the bottom of this. If it is true though, perhaps we can use it to our advantage. The more I think about it, my brain says that she certainly hasn't been very effective. And this tells me that Pope has not told her anything about our Manassas strategy. The Yanks wouldn't have charged into a trap had they known in advance that we knew the battle plan, and McDowell would be in jail."

"That is very true." Memminger responded. "Perhaps, when the time is right, we can say something seemingly innocuous, but totally wrong, in our next cabinet meeting, and then see if there is a Yankee response to the false seed we plant. Since she doesn't appear to have had any adverse impact on us, maybe Leroy is passing along conversational tidbits, but nothing of any substance."

"Excellent, yes, that is exactly what we shall do. Your son continues to impress, doesn't he?" Davis seemed to relax as he said that. "Ok, let's tackle fiscal policy. It's much more boring than talking about spies, wouldn't you say!"

The White House, August 30, 1861

President Lincoln sat with his cabinet during what had now become a weekly meeting. He had grown into the habit of allowing access to any of his cabinet members when they believed they needed access, or when he decided he required their presence. The only fixed date was that at 8 AM every Friday, the entire cabinet would meet upstairs in the White House. This was Friday, and they were meeting. They sat closely around a mahogany table the President Jefferson had used as a desk for one. When Lincoln had first seen it and it had been proposed as his cabinet meeting table, he simply said, "It will do." Then, he looked at Nicolay and whispered, "Do not let Mary know we will be meeting at this table. She will want to change it!" He didn't even comment on the chairs. They were small, and sat on rollers. His, at the head of the table, was the only one with arms. The whole set up led Lincoln to believe that at some point the table and chairs had been someone's dining room setup.

"Well, Mr. President, I know we have the drudgery of defeats to discuss, but before we do, I thought I may provide an update on events along the Virginia and Carolina coasts?" The speaker was Secretary of War Cameron.

"By all means", Lincoln replied with a wave of his hand.

"I love this story", Cameron continued. "We actually sent a naval officer up in a hot air balloon, tethered to our vessel, the 'Fanny'. He was able to get a full look at the reb positions around Hampton Road. They saw him and shot repeatedly at him." He chuckled. "The man was too high. They couldn't do anything to stop him from spying on their encampment. Although one musket ball actually landed in his basket, he was otherwise not threatened. When he went back the next day, they appear to have pulled back and moved down toward the Outer banks of the Carolinas."

"That is wonderful," said Lincoln. "What is this fellow's name?"

"John LaMountain, Sir. And even better, our boots on the ground tell us ole Beauregard ordered the troops to extinguish their fires that night. That means no hot chow. You know how well that is received by the rank and file! Also, I should report that General Butler, in partnership with the Navy, launched a combined ground and sea assault on Forts Hattaras and Clark along the Outer Banks. This happened yesterday, and we took the enemy by surprise and overwhelmed them. Those forts are now in our possession. We plan to slowly cut off the rebel's ability to conduct maritime trade."

The President sat up in his chair and looked slightly more animated. "Well, that is good news. At least someone out there is doing something! I hope McClellan is taking notes! And regards to that that Officer LaMountain, I will send him a letter of commendation. It's just that kind of ingenuity and bravery that will win us this infernal conflagration. Now, what is the bad news?"

Cameron cleared his throat and picked up a crystal ink holder Lincoln used for penning his letters and speeches. Even though the office Lincoln used faced north and there was no morning sun, the crystal still gleamed under the gas lights brightening the room. Cameron shook himself back to reality. "Yes, well, we lost General Nathaniel Lyon in Missouri, just outside Springfield on August 10. The rebs just flat out wore us down and we had to retreat. I'm afraid to say that defeat gives the enemy control of most of the state. I have no idea why it took so long for this news to get to me. We don't have this issue for matters here in the east."

Lincoln shook his head. "Well maybe that is because there is nothing happening here in the east!"

"There is more, Sir. I am told that General Fremont is considering taking an independent action and freeing all the slaves currently under confederate control in all of Missouri."

"He can't do that! He has no authority. If there is any question as to where loyalties lie in Missouri, that will push every last one of 'em into Jeff Davis's camp." Lincoln exclaimed, with a voice already raspy and fatigued.

"Yes, Sir. We have made our feelings known to the General. He has always been a bit bull-headed. Lastly, I understand from General McClellan that the Confederate Congress, at Jeff Davis's urging, is about to further divide duties between Generals Johnston and Beauregard and create five Brigadier Generals of equal standing. This will certainly not make either of those two very happy."

Secretary Chase asked, "Do we know who the other three are?"

"Yes, we do. According to McClellan's source, they will be Lee, Cooper, and Albert Johnston."

"Damn," said Lincoln. "I wanted Lee to stay with us. He's a good one." He leaned back, placed his hand on chin and mused, "I bet Washington and Jefferson are watching this whole debacle right now, and shaking their heads. They argued over states versus federal sovereignty issues eighty years ago, and here we are; same old, same old. At the end of the day, Lee chose his state over the Union. It's a powerful medicine, this state allegiance thing. And we lost many a good man to secessionist movement because of it."

The men around the table nodded their heads in agreement. They were not sycophantic nods; they were nods recognizing the truth in Lincoln's words. Lincoln continued, "I'm going to have to play the slavery card at some point during this whole mess. But I can't now. We'd pushed too many in the neutral camp to the wrong side. It's so confounding. I really don't think it's about slavery. I mean, how many people actually own slaves? Maybe 1% of the population? I mean, maybe not even 1%. And yet the 99% fight for a cause. That should be deeper. It's visceral. They just don't want to be told what to do, and they have this almost innate loyalty to their states. We just haven't done enough as a fledgling republic to promote the sense of unity. That is not on us, such as it is, gentlemen, but it is indeed our problem." Lincoln paused.

Attorney General Edward Bates did not usually say much, but

Lincoln was waxing philosophically in his domain; the constant strain between state and federal rights. "Indeed, Mr. President, indeed. You have hit the proverbial nail on the head. The whole slavery thing is a red herring. Of course, it is abhorrent. We all know it is long past an acceptable practice in a supposedly civilized society; centuries past if one is to look rationally at the issue. And we all know that the only ones who really care is the plantation class. Your one percent, as you referred to them, Sir.

You are right. We are fighting an enemy, the vast bulk of which could care less about slavery. But to your point, if you ever are to declare them free, they will then become competitors for jobs in the world of free men whose hearts and minds you are still trying to win. That, Sir, is what I call a conundrum."

Lincoln chuckled, "Edward, you have a way about you. Short and sweet; no mincing words. I appreciate your comments and I agree. I'm glad you are at the table, even if you did want my job. But then again, most of you in this room did, or still do!" Lincoln laughed again. The others also reared their heads back and guffawed. Lincoln wasn't sure they were all totally on his side yet, so in this case, he gave their guffaws a C+.

"But what to do, gentlemen, what to do? Greeley and the abolitionists want me to end slavery now. They think that is what this war is all about. I have made it so clear that this war is about the paramount goal of preserving the union. But let's face it, we need the support of everyone favoring those wearing blue uniforms, and we cannot afford to alienate any constituency."

Lincoln stood up and went over to a side table to pour himself a glass of water. He stood with his back to the table and looked at himself in the large mirror that was hung above a fireplace in the room. Lincoln turned around and continued. "Did you see the paper published this week by Frederick Douglass?" The facial expressions and movements around the table indicated that no one had. "Well, he wrote an account of the disaster that took place last month at Manassas. And guess what? He says there were a noticeable amount of colored soldiers fighting for the rebs." Several cabinet members' faces looked very surprised by that news. "Yessiree. Do you see the irony here? We have a view of these oppressed people, downtrodden, beaten, and depressed, in shackles. And of course no man should be enslaved by another. And yet, there they were, fighting in numbers alongside Johnny Reb. There is no indication they were fighting against their will. Yet we, I might add, have not allowed our free blacks to fight for the union. It just reinforces my view that this whole mess is about something far more visceral. None of us should delude ourselves. This is a battle for hearts and minds. It's not about slavery. Emancipation for our Negro slaves will be weapon I use at some point in the future to assist us in winning this war, and preserving our union. And of course, I will help close the ugly chapter in this book of our history. I believe it is called killing two birds with one stone. But now is not the time. Does anyone disagree?" His question was met by a silent chorus of heads shaking side to side.

"Right then, let's go back to General McClellan and this intelligence he is gathering. How did he know the rebs are about to promote Lee and the others?"

Cameron spoke after being a listener, laugher, and nodded for several minutes. "Well, Sir, it's quite a coincidence. My counterpart, Mr. Pope, whom I do not know, appears to have allowed himself to be tempted by a lady about town in Richmond. He and she are now engaged in what must be viewed as a good, old fashioned affair. I get the sense from McClellan that Pope is giving her conversational tidbits, but nothing of substance; at least not yet."

"Very good. Very good indeed," said the President. "Well let's see if she can work her wiles on him and get us some much-needed help. It almost feels to me as though they are a step ahead of us. Maybe this lady can help us to turn the tables. In any event, let's give Secretary

Seward an opportunity to fill us in on how our allies are responding to this situation. Then I want to hear, if you will indulge me, from Secretary Cameron and Chase regarding our military and supply build up and how on earth we will pay for it."

The meeting would last for several more hours. When it adjourned, Lincoln realized that while he was beginning to feel more comfortable with his cabinet, he had come to the conclusion that none of them liked each other very much, and many of them still wanted his job. After they left, he went off through the door next to the fireplace that led to his personal office.

"John?" The President spoke inquisitively as if to see if Nicolay was within earshot.

"Coming, Sir." While Nicolay's small office was adjacent to Lincoln's, he actually slept in the White House in what is presently called the Queen's Bedroom. Nicolay was never too far from Abe Lincoln. It's no wonder the book he would write one day in the future was so replete with intimate details. Latter day, readers would comment that it was as if he slept with the President. Well, he came darn close!

"I was just shipping Mrs. Lincoln off to New York, Sir. She boarded the train at Jersey Station about 45 minutes ago." (In 1861, the main station in Washington was Jersey Station. It was located about a block away, behind the Capital Building. It wasn't until 1907 that what we now know as Union Station was opened.) Nicolay had begun speaking as he walked down the hall from his room and finished as he entered the president's office. "Miss Chase sent me a note earlier and was planning to visit the White House around 5 PM."

"Hmmmm," the President grunted. "Well, that will be fine. We'll meet in the Red Room downstairs. Can't set the tongues wagging and hares running, now can we?"

"No, Sir, this would not do at all. I will make sure she is there," As it was already 4 PM, with the cabinet meeting having taken most of the day, Nicolay bade the President adieu and departed to prepare for another busy day.

As he was leaving, Lincoln yelled after him, "and John, let's get General McClellan in here at 9 AM tomorrow. That man is impossible. Haven't seen hide nor hair of him for too long."

"Yes Sir, will do," said Nicolay as his voice trailed off down the circular staircase.

Richmond, Virginia, September 5, 1861

Jeff Davis was sitting in his office with Confederate Attorney General Judah Benjamin. The AG was an accomplished lawyer, hailing originally from St. Croix, but spending most of his adult years in New Orleans, a city in which he obtained his law degree and built up a tidy fortune practicing his trade. He had then pursued politics and was a sitting US Senator before resigning to join the Confederacy. Perhaps more interesting was that fact that he was Jewish. Parenthetically, it was not lost on Lincoln that the northern cause, supposedly formed in the name of justice for all, had no blacks fighting for it, and no Jews in positions of prominence in the government. Yet the Confederacy did. Contradictions were rife!

It was a rainy day during early fall. The summer humidity had just begun to lift, but it was still relatively hot in Richmond. The average morning temperature was a pleasant 65 degrees and by 4 PM, it would rise to around 85. Benjamin lived relatively close to the Confederate headquarters and had taken a relaxing ten-minute walk over to meet his President.

"My thanks to you for coming over, Benjamin. There are a few things I'd like to cover. Um, did you get coffee?"

"Yes, Jeff, I believe it is coming in soon. Well, I must say I was curious when I received your summons. As you know, I haven't had much to do. We don't have courts, judges or a specific rule of law yet. I am AG of nothing."

"I know, I know", Davis responded, "But I wanted you in my cabinet, full stop. I want your mind close at hand. There will be other roles. Indeed, you are already providing me a huge service by seeing all these job seekers and keeping them off my back!" (As with Lincoln, there were no "firewalls" protecting the President Davis. Just about anyone could walk in off the street and seek time with him. From the day he had arrived in Richmond, Judah had agreed to have the "mob" diverted to him.) "I haven't thanked you appropriately for that. Anyway, I need your help and I need to know the conversation stays between us. May I trust that it will?" Benjamin nodded a yes. "Good. I don't know why I asked. I knew the answer. Anyway, we have a prickly situation that the Memmingers brought to me, and I want to use it to our advantage. I also want to do so in a way that no one besides you and I know what is happening." Benjamin looked intrigued.

"There is a lady here in town who has been seen in Washington by young Henry Memminger. That doesn't sound so bad by itself, but when you hear who he saw her with, you'll understand the importance. He saw her with McClellan."

Judah let out a "Well I'll be goldarned. We got ourselves a spy on our hands. I thought we were the only ones smart enough to have spies" he said jokingly.

Davis continued, "When Henry mentioned this, his father chimed in and allowed as to how he had come by information that our own Secretary of War, Mr. Pope, is having an affair with her!"

"Jiminy cricket! What else, is she sleeping with McClellan too!" Benjamin exclaimed.

"I have no idea, but what I do know is that you and I are going to lay a trap for Pope tomorrow in the Cabinet meeting, and no one, not even Chris, will know it is happening.

So here is what you will do. For whatever reason, nothing is happening on the war front. It's like everyone is taking a breather after a summer where best I can tell, most people were taking breathers! I want to plant a seed tomorrow and see how fast it gets back to McClellan."

Judah asked, "Do you think Pope is in on it?"

"No" replied Davis, "I just think he is just using his little head instead of the big one. Same mistake Adam made with Eve. But that said, the indiscretions are not acceptable, and once we prove what I already know we are going to prove, he will have to go. You know as well as I that there are many, myself included, who wished he had ordered Johnston and Beauregard to chase the yanks right back into the Capital after we whupped them at Manassas. I want a stronger leader for the war movement. I'm afraid Leroy is jus' a case of someone who shouldn't be runnin' with the big dogs cause he probably otta jus' stay under the porch."

"Why don't you get someone like Lee to come in from the field and take on that role?" Benjamin asked.

"That is brilliant, actually. And that kind of thought is why I need you close by my side. But no, we need Lee in the field. Mark my words, as this conflagration progresses, Lee will become an indispensable leader. No, Judah, I want you to keep your AG role, and also take on the War job."

Benjamin looked truly shocked. "Why, I am not a military man. For that matter, neither is Pope. Look how that has worked out for us!"

"You are right. But I am counting on two things. One, you will not act like a cad and engage in clandestine affairs, and two, you will use your brain to help me. I am afraid the stories of Mr. Pope's intellectual acumen were greatly exaggerated and he clearly is not up to the task. Don't worry, I will give him a military role somewhere where he can save face and not do any damage. He won't pitch a hissy fit. I reckon he'll be just fine; in fact, probably relieved."

"Jeff, if you want me to do it, I will. But I must tell you, my first reaction is one of concern. Part of that job should encompass the wisdom to tell you when you are wrong. From our few months together, I find we agree on most things almost like two brothers separated by a mother. What happens if we're both wrong? Neither of us know a darn thing about fightin' a war!"

"We'll jus' have to cross that bridge if and when we get to it. Now, let's talk about how we are going to solve our problem. Tomorrow, I was thinking you should mention how McClellan isn't doing a thing and while it is none of your business, maybe we should sneak our troops up toward Washington and position them for a strike. I will say, 'that is a great idea', or something like that, and then I'll ask Pope what he thinks." Davis had already placed a map on his desk and he picked it up to show Buchanan. He picked up his quill pen and pointed to Fredericksburg. "Johnston is already here with 10,000 men. That is 50 miles from Washington. I'm gonna suggest that he use stealth and move 5,000 of them 35 miles up the road to Alexandria. I'm gonna suggest he have them there no later than October 1. What can Pope say? We'll box him into a corner."

"I like it," said Buchanan. "But how will you manage to make sure Johnston doesn't take the order seriously?"

"If we are right, Pope will tell his lady friend, and she will get word to McClellan. He will immediately begin preparations for to move a force at least twice that size out of the Capital and toward Alexandria. It will all happen quickly. Johnston won't even have had time to get his supplies and logistics lined up. If it happens as we think, I'll relieve Pope, appoint you, and you can tell Johnston to stand down."

"There ya go again. I think its genius. That's why I am probably a horrible choice to replace Pope. What if yer just a dumbass and here I am agreeing 100% with you?"

"Ha, well if I turn out to be just a dumbass, then that just makes you one too!" Both men laughed. They talked about a few other things and the meeting adjourned.

The White House, September 12, 1861

President Lincoln was in his office when John Nicolay led General McClellan through the door. Lincoln stood up "Well, General, I have been anticipating your arrival ever since I received word during dinner last night that you needed to see me. I must say, I feel like I have had to pull teeth to get any of my generals to see me over the past few months, and here you are, standing in front of me of your own volition. It's a miracle, by jove!"

The General stood ramrod straight, still in the doorway, in his dress blues.

"Is there an occasion, General? You seem dressed to the nines."

"A man slovenly in appearance is slovenly in action, Sir."

"Well then, if the opposite holds true, we will certainly slay the foe in the field when we finally see some action, won't we General!" Lincoln chuckled, kicking himself that even while he spoke to McClellan he could not shake his very own description of the man as a popinjay. The General remained ramrod straight. "Oh for heaven's sake General, have a seat and tell me why you have come to see me. Even generals can take a little joshin', can't they?"

"Umm, yes Sir. Of Course, Sir." McClellan finally broke his formal stance as Lincoln motioned for him to sit in the chair across from his desk. "Mr. President, I have it upon very good advice that the rebs are planning a surprise assault upon us here in the capital." Lincoln's eyebrows rose until they almost touched his hairline. "General Johnston is, at this very moment, moving 5,000 troops up the Turnpike to Alexandria. He is going to great lengths to keep the mission under wraps. I'm told that he believes he will not need large numbers if he can cross the Potomac and catch us sleeping."

"My goodness" said the President. "It sounds just like what good 'ole Sam Houston did to Santa Anna down there in that swamp in Texas. He surely proved one can overpower an enemy if one has the element of surprise on his side. Are you sure of this, General?"

"My source is impeccable. I am coming to seek your permission to quietly move a considerably larger force over the river and to place them north and west of Alexandria. When Johnston arrives, we can pinch him against the Potomac and deal a devastating blow."

"I'm all in General! You hardly expected me to say 'no', did you? Go with God's speed man. By all means, have everything in place before the rebs get there. And please, please, keep your plans tight. We have too many loose lips in this town. Let's set a new precedent for this war, and actually gain the upper hand through stealth and discretion."

McClellan stood and headed toward the door. Once there, he turned and saluted the President crisply. "Sir, I believe this is the advantage we have been looking for. The troops are not nearly battle-ready, but with the element of surprise, we stand a chance of smoking the enemy right into the river."

"Go with God, General, go with God." Lincoln waved him off and sat back down. Just as he heard the General's footsteps receding down the staircase, he heard Mary's familiar patter coming down the hall from the living quarters.

"Abe", she said as she walked in, "we have hardly seen each other or spoken these last few days since I returned from New York. How are you? Is the effort moving along?"

"Well Mary, the last we spoke my bowels were a bit tied up. That effort?" He asked with a twinkle in his eye.

"Oh Abraham Lincoln, you rascal. No, not that! My heavens, if that hadn't sorted itself out you would have exploded by now. You're all skin and bones. You haven't any room in there for things to hang around too long on the inside!"

Lincoln laughed. "So tell me about your trip to New York. It is a city I care little about, as they are not kind to me, but in truth, Mary, we need all those Irish and German immigrants to join big blue!"

"Oh Abe, I know Mr. Greeley has been harsh. But I do believe it is because he is so single-minded about the slavery debate. He doesn't see the big picture as you always have. You must forgive him for that. But New York, oh, what a marvelous city. It stretches from Wall Street up and up and up. I was given a tour and the streets, oh, so many of them, well, they are confusing in the old part of the city…little cobblestone streets with no rhyme or reason…but then these large avenues begin and they head straight north, and then there are numbered streets running east and west. Those immigrants you mentioned live horribly in areas in the lower numbered streets."

Mary was talking a mile a minute. She was just getting warmed up. Lincoln listened and was enjoying her ramble. "And then Abe, as we headed north to, oh, I think about 34th Street, things started opening up and before I knew it I was in farmland! Can you believe it? I went from our biggest city to farms in the blink of an eye. And you know what I saw?" Lincoln looked at her inquisitively.

"I'll tell you what I saw. There was a marker on a farm 2 or 3 miles north of 34th Street on the east side of the island, and it said 'This is the tree where the British forces hung American patriot Nathan Hale for acts of treason.' Oh Abraham, so much history there in New York. I absolutely loved it."

"Mary, it sounds as though you had a grand old time. Now please don't ruin it by telling me you shot right through our new White House expense budget for furnishings and the like."

Mrs. Lincoln chuckled. "No, you would have been proud of me. I actually only bought a bed. We so need a bed for that bedroom across from Mr. Nicolay's, so we can put up family members and friends when they come to stay in a little more comfort. It's a very nice bed." (The irony was horrible. The room to which she made reference would, in time, become known as The Lincoln Bedroom. The President, to the best of our knowledge, never slept in that room. The mattress on the bed, however, is rumored to have lasted all the way until Barbara Bush changed it out for something newer and more comfortable!) Those lucky enough to stay in that room during the future terms of myriad presidents would not be able to ignore the history and even more fascinating, they were fortunate enough to see an actual handwritten version of what would become one of Mr. Lincoln's most famous speeches; the Gettysburg Address.)

"Hah, only a bed? Well, then I consider this trip to be an enormous success Mary. Well done you!" Lincoln exclaimed.

"There is more, Abraham. I also had the opportunity to meet Frederick Douglass at the Astor House. I told you I stayed there, yes?" Lincoln gave her a silent, affirmative nod. "Well, I know you have seen it, because you told me you stayed there last year. Oh, it is magnificent, and only a short walk from City Hall. Well, it is central to everything. I suppose it won't be some day, if that city keeps growing the way it is, but right now, well, it is the nicest hotel I have ever seen."

"I have to agree with you Mary, it is quite a place. Tell me about your meeting with Douglass."

"Yes, yes, oh what a remarkable man. He is so well spoken, and so committed to his cause. But he is reasonable Abraham. I told him we had slaves in our family back in Kentucky, and we considered them family. He asked me why if we considered them family didn't we free them and let them decide themselves whether they wanted to be part of the family. I thought that was such an odd question, and I just said 'Mr. Douglass, that just isn't something we would do, and I don't think our slaves would want us to. Well, he was polite, but it was very clear he didn't agree with me. You know, he was a slave just down the road near Baltimore, and he escaped when he was twenty years old. When he was finally free, he said he was so poor he couldn't afford to pay attention to how poor he was! I thought that was a lovely expression. Anyway, he wished to meet you someday hence."

Mary stopped and took a breath. Lincoln filled the empty air. "Mary, it sounds all in all as though you had a wonderful trip. I am happy for you. I also would be pleased to meet with Frederick Douglass. By all accounts he is a remarkable man."

Mary got up to leave, and said, "My only complaint about New York is that some of them just aren't very polite. They speak fast, and they have funny accents. I guess if that is my only complaint, then that is pretty good, right?"

Lincoln laughed again. "I'd say we can forgive them for their brusqueness. I have never heard anything but that about New Yorkers, and I suspect it will ever be thus."

"Dinner at 7, Abraham" Lincoln heard her say as she walked back toward the living quarters.

Mary Surrat Boarding House, Washington, D.C., September 13, 1861

Henry Memminger had surreptitiously found his way back into Washington and thanks to some advice given him back in Richmond, was safely ensconced within the walls of Mary Surrat's Boarding House on H Street. Mary lived a non-descript life, and probably would have until her natural dying day. She was, however, a southern sympathizer and would routinely house travelers sympathetic to that cause throughout the war. The mistake that would ultimately lead to her ruin was several years later, when she hosted the conspirators involved with President Lincoln's assassination. That event led to her being sentenced to death by hanging. Her name lives in infamy as the first female ever sentenced to death by hanging in the United States. But all that was a few years away. At this moment in time, no one in Washington was the wiser, and Henry found himself in a safe haven.

As he sat at the breakfast table, Mary brought him coffee, followed by scrambled eggs, bacon, toast, and grits. Among other things, she was a handy cook.

"Word in my circles is that you have served President Davis admirably." She said as she sat down to eat with him. "Do you know about Rose O'Neal Greenhow?"

Henry looked at her quizzically. "No, ma'am, I do not."

"Well, Henry, she is in jail now, and can you guess why? The yanks think she passed information along to General Beauregard regarding troop movements before the Bull Run battle. But we know better, don't we?" She looked at him and winked. "All the same, that poor lady is in for a rough time. I feel bad for her."

"I don't know her, and I hadn't heard that story." Henry said, holding a fork full of scrambled eggs, and bouncing it up and down. His appetite was suddenly quenched.

"Well, Henry, if I were you, I would skedaddle. The yanks know about you and there's plenty of 'em who wouldn't mind givin' you a good whuppin'."

Memminger paused, and sat back in his chair. It creaked as though it may break, so he slowly leaned forward, and looked around the room before talking. It was a breakfast enclave that did not distinguish itself from thousands of others around the country. A round table, with a lazy Susan in the center. There was jam, butter, honey, salt and pepper on it. A gas-lit chandelier was above it, and a woven cotton rug was beneath. Linen curtains hung on the one window, which looked out on to H Street. The morning sun poured through that window and Henry could see it was softening the butter on the lazy Suzan to perfection. He took his knife and carved a nice slice to apply to his toast. Then, having applied some peach preserves, he took a bite and looked back at Miss Surrat.

"Lazy Susans are a product of American ingenuity. So simple, so practical" He said. "Did you know Thomas Jefferson made the first one, because his young daughter could never reach what she wanted on the table? He was something." Mary Surrat smiled. He continued, "Yes, Miss Surrat, you are right. I do need to make myself scarce in this town. There is just some activity I am noticing and I need to get to the bottom of, and if I can figure out what is happening, believe you me, I will skedaddle, just as you suggest!"

"That's good Henry. You are a good young man, and you need to look after yourself. And speaking of that, if it isn't too personal, do you have any love in your life?"

Henry looked at her, and couldn't tell whether that was a backhanded proposal to turn his stay into something more than what it was. He responded with the truth quickly, which, regardless of the intention behind her question, would provide the necessary answer. "I do indeed, Miss Surrat. She is a wonderful girl in Richmond, although originally from South Carolina. I hope to marry her someday."

Miss Surrat's face lit up. She looked genuinely happy for him. "That is so nice to hear. You be good to her, and you will live a long, happy life. But if ya really love her, stop piddlin' around and pop the question!"

"Yes ma'am", he laughed, "I aim to do just that soon enough."

After breakfast, Henry meandered to the west where troops were bivouacked. He had seen an unusual amount of activity the last forty-eight hours. He wore his army uniform that had helped him gain entrance to General McDowell's house some two months back. The uniform was a double-edged sword. It certainly gave him free rein to walk about town. At the same time, he ran the risk of a senior officer asking him who he was, what he was doing, and why he wasn't with his brigade. He had answers ready for those questions, but he preferred not to be asked.

The sun that had shone through the window during breakfast at Mary Surrat's was now covered by what looked to be cumulous rain clouds. Henry wanted to make quick work of his time near the union army, and doubly, he would just as soon not get soaked by the rain that seemed headed his way. He breathed in hard through his nose. There are those times when one can almost smell rain before it actually arrives. This was one of those times.

As he neared the Potomac, he saw acres of union encampments and much hustle and bustle. He looked on the fringe of all the activity for a private; someone who would pay him the respect due the lieutenant's bars on his uniform. He saw just the prospect he was seeking some fifty feet in front of him. The private was on his knees, attempting to cram his eating materials into a knapsack, and tie all that below his sleeping bag. The goal was to have one tight package across his back that would stay in place for a long march.

"Good day Private" Henry said.

The private leapt to his feet and saluted Henry. He didn't look like he could have been more than 16 years old, and he spoke with a very heavy Irish accent. "Good day to ya, Sir. Top o' the morning to you as well."

"Who is your commander, son?"

"Well blimey if I know Sir, beggin' your pardon of course, Sir. All I know is that Seargent McPhearson over there told us to get ready to do some marching and fight some rebels."

Henry chuckled "A Scotsman giving you orders. Can you understand him?"

With this, the private laughed in return, and said, "As well as he can understand me Sir!"

"You look like you are headed yonder over the river" Henry spoke.

"Yes sir, we are told Johnny reb is trying to sneak up and catch us sleeping. Some place called Alexandria, or something like that."

"Oh, I hadn't heard that. Well, you won't have long to march. It's not far the other side of the bridge. You take care private. War isn't all that fun."

"Yes sir. I appreciate that Sir. I get a hot meal every day, and that is better than I ate back in Ireland."

"Godspeed, Private." With that Henry turned and ambled slowly back in the direction of Mary Surrat's boarding house. He would wait until it was dark, take his horse, and hightail it back to Richmond. Without interruption, he would be there by the 16th.

As Henry was walking back to gather his things and wait for dark, General McClellan was meeting with Generals Nathaniel Banks and Fitz-john Porter. He had brought them into the plan a day before he met with Lincoln. Word was already seeping into the rank and file. It seemed nigh impossible to keep any secret at all.

"Gentlemen", McClellan began, "I am disturbed to learn that our plans are already making their way through the encampment. Be that as it may, let's make haste. I want to be across the bridge tomorrow. Are we all clear on duties? Fitz, you stake out the position in the north, and Banksee, you cover the western flank." McClellan liked giving nicknames to his subordinates. In a way, it was the only endearing thing he might ever have done. "It looks like rain, so let's move with dispatch. I know it sound ironic coming from me. I'm quite aware everyone thinks I prefer to move with the snails, not dispatch! Well, I told the President we are not ready. But this is too good an opportunity to pass on. Let's strike a blow."

The plans were set. The union troops would begin moving within the hour.

CHAPTER SEVEN
ANOTHER BLOW

Richmond, Virginia, September 16, 1861

Henry had travelled over 70 miles as the crow flies, but much more in reality. He could not afford to be seen by pickets on either side of the fight. During his trip to Richmond, he thought of a poem that had been written that month. It addressed the lack of major battles while all along people were dying. Written by Ethyl Lynn Beers, a yank, it resonated throughout both the blue and grey troops. Part of it read:

"All quiet along the Potomac," they say,

"Except now and then a stray picket

Is shot, as he walks on his beat, to and fro,

By a rifleman hid in the thicket.

'Tis nothing-a private or two, now and then,

Will not count in the news of the battle."

It wasn't hard to see why Henry thought of those lyrics as he weaved a course toward safety in Richmond.

He walked up the steps of the townhouse and entered the headquarters where it seemed Jefferson Davis almost always was. By happenstance, when he was shown into the office which now was quite familiar to him, he saw Judah Benjamin, his father, and

President Davis. The President was at his desk, with his father and Benjamin in chairs directly across from and facing their boss.

"The Prodigal son returns!" Exclaimed Davis. "What news have you? Criminy, you look like hell." He motioned Henry to pick up a chair and put it next to his father. They all sat down.

"I got here as fast as I could Mr. President. I do have news. Unbeknownst to me, I guess you have ordered General Johnston to work his way up to Alexandria and plan a sneak attack on Washington. Unfortunately, Sir, the yanks know, and they are laying a trap as I speak. I hope it's not too late."

Davis and Benjamin smiled. Chris Memminger looked horrified. As he took their reactions in, Henry just looked perplexed. "Sirs, I am clearly missing something."

"You are not alone, son." Christopher Memminger spoke in such a way that it was more of a question directed at Davis than a statement to his son.

Davis broke the tension. "Sometimes in matters of state and war, discretion is the better part of valor. Even though you two alerted me to the spy in our midst-right in our midst considering her relationship with Secretary Pope-I felt that secrecy was paramount. I had to find out whether it was true. So Jonah and I fabricated a battle plan and the cabinet, including Secretary Pope, agreed it. We couldn't even tell General Johnston, but we managed it so that he will have wasted preparation time and may now be a few miles out of Richmond, but we will call him back."

Memminger the father looked at the President and Jonah. "So there is no march to Alexandria, and you have proven that we do indeed have a leak through Pope?"

"Yes. He is a good man, but in over his head, and now we know he is way too indiscreet. He means us no harm, but he doesn't

111

understand the forces at work against us. He will be relieved of his duties today, and I will send him somewhere south; as a general and with a remit to do absolutely nothing. He will understand."

"Wow", said Henry; it was an expression he had picked up at Harvard.

Davis looked at him. "Son, you have worked miracles again. The yanks are running around like chickens with their heads cut off, and all they are doing is chasing ghosts. Ole' Abe will be furious." He guffawed.

Chris Memminger asked, "Since you figured all this out, you no doubt also have a new Secretary of War?"

"He is on your right," Davis said, pointing at Mr. Benjamin. "You are looking at him."

The elder Memminger could not hide his surprise. Jonah laughed, and said, "It's ok Chris, I agree with you. But our President is quite insistent, and of course, I have given him my word I will do everything in my power to assist the cause."

Washington, D.C.
October 23, 1861

The President, Secretary Cameron, and General McClellan were in a field on the outskirts of town, looking out over the Potomac. With them was a spry man, with a strong European accent. He was there to demonstrate a new weapon; a machine gun. His name was Agar, and the gun was of Swiss design. When he let it fly over the Potomac, Lincoln and the others were very impressed. It shot 120 rounds in a minute.

Lincoln immediately ordered the purchase of ten of them, and more orders followed during the war.

Lincoln had taken the opportunity to walk the 2 miles to the testing site, and looked forward to walking back. Good ole Popinjay had ridden out with a phalanx of soldiers surrounding him. As Lincoln turned to walk back, he said, "General, why don't you have your men take your horse back. You, Secretary Cameron and I can walk and catch up." Lincoln knew it was the last thing McClellan wanted to do, but he really didn't care.

McClellan, accepting his fate, motioned to one of the horse guard to take the reins of his horse. "Take care of Daniel Webster, private." The private nodded in ascent and drew the horse away.

"Daniel Webster," said the President. "Why that is a fine name. He was, by all accounts, a very good man. Quite a vocabulary I hear. Someone told me the Supreme Court dreaded him coming in for an argument because he always used words they had to look up!"

"Yes, Mr. President. He is my favorite horse, and I hope to do well in his namesake's honor."

"Admirable, General, admirable." They had begun the walk back toward the White House. He changed subjects. "General, first, let me congratulate you and your wife on the birth of your daughter. These are trying times, no doubt, but it will give you solace knowing you are trying to make the world a better place for your young baby."

"Thank you, Sir. She is a little angel."

"Now, the Secretary and I could not help but notice your rather conspicuous absence since whatever that disappointment was across the river in Alexandria. Perhaps you could fill us in."

"Yes, well, um, it appears my source was not as impeccable as I had thought. You see, gentlemen, I was in contact with a lady from Richmond who managed to ingratiate herself to secretary Pope. She was becoming a valuable asset. She informed me of Johnston's plans to make a move on the capital."

Cameron spoke up, "Pray tell, General, what happened?"

The men had left the soggy ground near the river and were now walking through Union army encampments. Their presence was causing quite a stir. There were thousands of soldiers milling about, but one could sense a buzz of excitement as they proceeded through the camp. It is quite possible that McClellan and Cameron could have walked through the tents and training areas with salutes and some fanfare. But Abe Lincoln was an entirely different story. Standing 6'4" tall, he towered above all other men. There was no way he was going to walk around in broad daylight without drawing attention to himself. The conversation was stalled for no other reason than the tremendous groundswell of cheers coming from the men in front of them. Troops from left and right were running to catch a glimpse of Old Abe. And much to McClellan's horror, they began chanting his name. "Lincoln, Lincoln, Lincoln!" They cheered and banged pots together and did just about whatever they could to make noise. It was a downright cacophony.

Lincoln knew he could not just keep walking and tipping his stovepipe hat. "Excuse me gentlemen. I think this moment merits some comments." The President may not have been the smoothest of politicians, but he knew a good opportunity when he saw one. Leaping up on a wagon near the path they had been on, he took his hat off to talk. There were now some 1,000 soldiers pressing in on him. When they saw him jump up on the wagon, they exploded with cheers.

Lincoln took it all in for about twenty seconds, and then used his arms to calm them down. Eventually they were quiet enough for him to talk. "Men of the Army of the Potomac. I am so proud of you. Your country is proud of you. You know, I know many of you were not even born in these United States. But you came for a better opportunity, and now you find yourselves fighting to make sure you have a chance for that opportunity. God Bless you." The troops clapped and cheered, and Lincoln quieted them down again. "Soldiers, I know you are bored and want to take it to the enemy. Why, that is exactly why I am here talking to General McClellan. Say, who is ready for some action?!" The crowd of blue-clad troops went crazy with excitement. When they calmed down again, Lincoln concluded, "That is what I thought!" And with a big smile, he said, "Well, let's see if we can come up with some plans to get you into the battle. What do you say?" The troops erupted once again. Lincoln waved to them all, stepped down from the ladder, and he, Cameron, and the General went forward into the sea of blue.

Having finally emerged on the other side, and leaving the chorus of cheers behind, Lincoln resumed. "Apologies, Gentlemen. It needed to be done. General you certainly have some eager troops on your hands. Perhaps they should be granted their wish, heh? In any event, I think Secretary Cameron had just asked what happened to your lady spy, and why were we hoodwinked yet again?"

McClellan walked with two of his brass buttons undone, and his right hand tucked in over his stomach. It reminded Lincoln of sketches he had seen of Napoleon Bonaparte. It was not a comparison Lincoln wanted to make. "Yes, indeed. In point of fact Sirs, it appears we were double-crossed. I am told my contact has been arrested, and Secretary Pope, in fact, has resigned, and accepted a general's title in the army. He apparently will be assigned to some outpost in the deep south."

Cameron spoke, "So the entire exercise was a ruse?"

"Apparently it was." General McClellan looked off into the distance, clearly uncomfortable coming face to face with the fact that he and his army had been tricked into pursuing a fool's errand. "But Mr. President, I fear you see these forces here in the capital and assume nothing is happening. We have troops out west, down south along the coast, and early next year we aim to take the ports of New Orleans and Galveston. We are moving according to plan, Sir. We are winning, Sir."

"Mmmmm", said Lincoln. "Tell me, General, about how many contacts resulting in battles of any nature have we had since Fort Sumpter?"

"Oh, I don't know exactly Sir. I would venture to say around twenty."

"Well, I will tell you exactly how many General. Including Fort Sumpter, we have engaged or been engaged by the enemy twenty-four times. And guess what? Putting a realistic light on things, we can say we did not lose half the time. Half! And just two days ago, in Balls Bluff Virginia, did we not just lose nearly 600 men when they surrendered to the rebs?"

"Yes, Mr. President, that is accurate."

"So, General, I do not think I am making myself clear, although for the life of me I believe I have been very, very clear. Don't get me wrong. I am pleased that we have troops spreading across our land and there is a grand plan. But General, nothing is happening! And when it does happen, we lose half the time! Now tell me, in a war when one side wins only half the time, what happens?"

"Sir, is that a rhetorical question?" General McClellan looked at the President, and Lincoln could not tell whether he was mocking him.

"General, you are a student of military history. You must be. You went to West Point. I'm sure you know what happened in the years 1337-1453?" Lincoln's eyes bored into McClellan's, and the General averted Lincoln's penetrating glare and looked ponderously up at the sky. "It is what is now known as the Hundred Years' War. The English won big battles and so did the French. But neither side was able to vanquish the other. For over a hundred years! Generations of families came and went and the same war was being fought. It can happen General. Do you understand? This cannot happen here!"

"Mr. President, I am doing all I can do."

The three of them were now approaching the south side of the White House. Lincoln could tell that McClellan would have given just about anything to beat a hasty retreat from this conversation. Lincoln had removed his coat and was just wearing his typical white shirt, the likes of which he had worn nearly every day since he had established a law practice back in Illinois. Cameron was perspiring. There was a fall chill in the air, but the pace had been brisk once they had left the encampment behind. McClellan had shed nothing. He remained fastidiously dressed, with nothing out of place. Lincoln stopped on Pennsylvania Avenue, knowing that McClellan would veer off there.

"General. I am sorry if I am making you uncomfortable. I know you are a patriot. What I am trying to say is that we must use the resources at our disposal and take the fight to the enemy. I would be a rich man if I had a dollar for every time I have said 'time is their ally, not ours.' I know you think it is the opposite. Our blockades are starting to work. They already are having trouble exporting cotton and other materials to Europe. They do not have access to our manufacturing capabilities. But General, if we let them build strength and defenses, we will make this war a horrible, long, drawn out affair. We cannot let that happen. Do we understand each other?"

McClellan sighed, and said, "Yes, Mr. President, I understand you. War is complicated. That is why you have men like me to help you."

Cameron touched Lincoln's arm, just to make sure the President didn't lose his composure. He needn't have worried. No one ever saw Lincoln lose control in public. It was an amazing attribute. Lincoln looked at his popinjay, and calmly said, "You should do something about your boots soldier. They got quite muddy during our walk." As he finished his sentence, he turned and walked toward the people's house; his house; the White House. Left alone, McClellan looked down at his boots, and was horrified. If there was anything Winfield Scott, old Fuss and Feathers, had taught him, it was that a soldier must always look perfect.

117

Lincoln said goodbye to Secretary Cameron at the door, and entered the ground floor of the White House. John Nicolay greeted him in the long hallway inside. "General Scott is waiting for you in the Green Room Sir."

Lincoln took that in stride, and asked, "Any idea what this is about, John?"

"No Sir. I explained you were out with General McClellan. He said he would wait. He has been in there for about an hour and a half. Not to worry, though; the chef gave him a couple ham sandwiches and a glass of wine. And I gave him the papers for the day."

Lincoln grunted and followed John up the stairs to the first floor. They remained silent until entering the Green Room.

"Don't get up, General." Lincoln spoke as he entered the room. Nicolay took an unassuming seat in the corner. Lincoln went over to the General, who had not made any effort to stand in any event, and shook his hand. "I hope you are well. It is good to see you. I miss our visits."

"Thank you for asking Mr. President. All things considered, I am fine. I am old, I have gout, and I feel useless. Other than that, just fine." Of course, what he didn't say is that he had done everything he could do during the very earliest days of the war to slow the President's plans down.

"I am sorry I've kept you waiting. I understand how frustrated you must feel. Although really General, if you have been following events, as I am sure you have, you haven't missed very much!"

General Scott laughed. "Well, I guess you are right about that, Mr. President." And then, seizing on the opportunity to make one more contribution to the southern cause, he said, "Mr. President, I know you probably don't want to hear this, but I really think you should consider suing for peace. Surely we can develop a very strong

118

relationship with the southern states. We would save so much bloodshed. And the two countries could go on about their respective businesses; separate, but equal."

Lincoln looked long and hard at the General. "You are not wrong General. It seems this is going to be a long, bloody affair; a human tragedy. But you couldn't be more wrong regarding that which you suggest. Ours is a noble democratic republic; unlike any that has come before. We cannot let this secession stand. Nothing, and I mean nothing, is more important than the preservation of our union. It may not be the expedient path. It may be a horrible journey. But it is the right thing to do, and I am hell-bent to see it through."

"I knew you would say that Mr. President, but I felt it necessary to try. In any event, I came to tell you I am resigning my commission. I am 75, and past my sell-by date. This is no secret to anyone. I should tell you Sir, that I hear tell that General McClellan has suggested that I may be a spy for the opposition."

"There is too much scuttlebutt General. You have served your country well, and Lord knows you've seen so much of our young country's growth. You deserve a break. What will you do?"

"I have secured a small house in West Point, and will spend the rest of my years there, where I formed so many lifetime friendships. Alas, so many good men, many from the south. But West Point is the glue that holds us all together. It is our bond."

"I understand General. I guess that means I will formally elevate General McClellan to lead our entire army. I cannot tell you that makes me comfortable; not by any stretch. I wish you were twenty-five years younger. I cannot help but feel that you would be leading us to success more, how shall I say, maybe 'energetically' than others seem to be doing. In any event General, I assume we should make this announcement soon?"

"I was thinking November 1ˢᵗ, Sir."

"Then that day it shall be. If nothing else, we know that General McClellan will be most pleased!"

The White House, December 24, 1861

The President stood in the family dining room, looking out the window. He was thinking about the year that had transpired. It seemed like an eternity since he had been sworn into office. So much water under the bridge; so much water still flowing toward him and his quest to save the union known as the United States of America.

He was as relaxed as he could be, given the circumstances. It had been nearly seven weeks since he appointed General McClellan as what amounted to the supreme commander of the US Army. Virtually nothing had happened. Yes, the same could be said for the rebels. They too seemed mired in mud of their own making. But that didn't make Lincoln feel any better. As he had thought and said innumerable times, it was incumbent on the army of the north to be the aggressor. And it just wasn't happening.

This night, though, was Christmas Eve. His son Robert was home for Christmas; having just finished his first semester as a freshman at Harvard. Then there was eleven-year old Willie, and eight year old Tad. Lincoln was looking forward to spending some time with Robert. His was a childhood that Lincoln largely missed. He had been on his horse pursuing his legal trade for most of Robert's childhood. The two had never grown close.

Joining them at the family's Christmas Eve dinner was Mary's half-sister, Emilie. She had traveled in from Kentucky at Mary's invitation. Her husband would not be joining the family, because he had chosen to take up arms against the north. It was, unfortunately, hardly a unique situation. The Civil War between the States often pitted family member against family member. In this case, Emilie's husband, Ben Helm, had attended West Point, and was a rising star in the army. When hostilities broke out, Lincoln actually offered him the job of Paymaster General; thus securing a senior position, and simultaneously assuring he would be away from the heat of battle. After much hand wringing, Helm had decided his loyalties were to the south, and he joined the secessionist cause. As a consequence, Emilie, of whom both Lincoln and Mary were very fond, found herself traveling alone to Washington for a family dinner.

Lincoln heard voices behind him and realized the family was gathering in the living room. He turned to join them, noticing that all but Tad were present and already seated. He actually had not yet seen Emilie, so he walked over and the two embraced. "It is so good to see you, young Emilie. I am just so sorry we do not have Ben here also."

"Oh Abe, I know. He just couldn't do it. I don't even know where he is at the moment. But I pray he is well, and I pray even harder we will be united as a family whatever may come of this mess."

With that they all heard young Tad's voice coming up the stairs to the living quarters. "Hut, one, two, three four. Hut, one, two, three four." And so on. Lincoln looked quizzically toward the top of the stairs. Tad appeared, followed by two of the army privates who were stationed at the White House front door. Tad led them into the living room and then turned to face them. "Ten hut!" He shouted to the two soldiers. They came to full attention, staring into an abyss that was in reality the entire Lincoln family.

"Tad, will you please explain yourself?" Lincoln inquired.

"Dad, these men looked bored and I thought it would do them some good to practice their marching."

Robert laughed, and when he did, the rest of the family did. Well, all but the President. "Tad, you are not an officer of my army. You have no authority to tell these men to march upstairs and stand at attention. Do you understand me, son?"

Tad then faced his father, stood ramrod straight, looked him in the eye, saluted, and said "Yes, Sir!" the family laughed again, and discernible smiles were on both faces of the soldiers.

Lincoln looked at the two privates. "You two are dismissed, and Mrs. Lincoln and I apologize on behalf of our son." Both soldiers saluted, did an about face, and moved toward the staircase. They could be heard laughing as they descended the flight of stairs.

"It's a good thing we have great young men serving this army. What on earth were you thinking, son?"

"Ah, pa, I was just havin' fun." The boy looked imploringly up at his dad. "Tad, you disrespected those two men. And even though they took it well, you need to apologize to them tomorrow. You need to show some character."

"OK, I will. But what is character?"

Lincoln laughed. "Character is like a tree and reputation is its shadow. The shadow is what we think it is and the tree is the real thing."

Tad looked perplexed. Mary broke into the conversation and said, "Let's all go into dinner, shall we?"

Richmond, Virginia, December 24, 1861

Christopher and Mary Memminger were excited that the Frank family had permitted their Janie to join Henry and them for Christmas Eve dinner at their Richmond residence. It was an evening to which all of them had been looking forward. Mary was particularly excited; she had never seen Henry so excited about a girl, and she knew he was in love. Chris had been having an increasingly difficult time in his capacity as Secretary of the Treasury. He knew in his heart the only way he was funding the war effort was due to southern forces having confiscated the union's gold deposits in New Orleans. Once that gold was gone, there was nothing backing the issuance of confederate currency besides faith. Jeff Davis told him "Chris, you have to work your magic. Faith works in churches; people need more than faith to know the paper in their pockets will be worth something."

Memminger had been busy trying to sell bonds, and putting the machinery in place to print currency. He was very, very nervous about the potential inability of his government to fund a long, protracted war, and he had every reason to be.

The Memminger household was a normal one for the upper-crust of Richmond society. That is another way of saying that they had a couple slaves living under their roof. One of them was named Sally. Her mother had worked on their property in South Carolina. She had never known her father. Mary Memminger had taught her to read and write. She also had gotten to know Varina Davis, wife of the President, Jefferson Davis. Ironically, Varina was outspokenly anti-slavery, and at best, ambivalent about the war effort. She was not, and never would be, an advocate for secession. Sally wasn't unhappy. She had a roof over her head, no expenses, and a family that treated her nicely. She had freedom to move around town during the day, and, other than the occasional derogatory and wholly uncalled for remark from some random passerby, (usually because of her attractiveness) no one bothered her.

On this Christmas Eve, she was in charge of ensuring the dinner was cooked to perfection and the presentation was performed without a flaw. So, while she was completely content in performing that role, she was the most surprised when, after dinner, Mary Memminger invited her to join them at the table. As nice as the Memminger's were, this just wasn't done. Mary had an ulterior motive. She was testing Janie to see how she would react. Janie passed the test with flying colors. In fact, after having been asked to join them, and standing awkwardly while digesting the invitation, Janie was the one to break the silence by putting her hand on the cushion of the dining room table beside her and said "Yes, Sally, please sit here. I bet you and I are about the same age. It is wonderful to be able to get to know you better." Case closed. Janie was a keeper.

The Memminger house was a classic Richmond brick Georgian four story townhouse. Richmond was long regarded by the British as that town that most resembled west London. The houses were well built, similar looking, and populated by people who looked the same!

The dining room in which they now sat had all the modern gas lighting appliances, but they were only on the walls. A beautiful old school candle-lit chandelier was above the imported mahogany table. The conversation that ensued was relaxed and there was little to no tension, even with Sally at the table. At one point, Henry asked her, "So Sally, from your perspective, what do you think of this war?" A hush swept through the room. It was a question, the answer to which could go in any number of directions.

Sally smiled and looked at each of those sitting around the table. "Henry, I cry at night when I think of where all this is headed. I do not see any outcome that is better for my people, and I fear for you and your family, and others like you. I do not see how anything good comes of this."

Henry looked at her, knowing that his mother and father and most likely Janie were doing the same. "Well, Sally, that is a short and sweet answer. And I understand it. I dare say father does too. We have taken on a steep mountain to climb, and the path to the top is anything but clear. I guess only God knows. But we have crossed the divide, and the bridge that existed has been demolished. There is only one way to go and that is forward. I hope for all our sakes God is just, and God is on our side."

Sally looked at him and said "Amen, Henry, Amen. I just worry when I read that Mr. Lincoln is also praying that God is just and that he is on the Union side. God certainly has a lot of people praying that he is on their side!" With that, everyone had a laugh. Christopher Memminger lifted his glass and said "A very Merry Christmas to us all. And God, if you are listening, we could use a little help!" If it is true that all is well that ends well, then this Christmas Eve dinner ended well.

Henry and Julia put their overcoats on and left to begin the three-block walk to Julia's parent's house. Walking arm in arm down the gas-lit streets, Julia looked up at Henry and said "You know I love you Henry Memminger." It was a statement, not a question.

"I would never take you for granted, so even if I did think I knew that, I would never admit it" Henry said, laughing.

"I have been thinking", she said, "That I want to help you. I want to help your father, and I want to help all of us win this war." Henry stopped and looked at her.

"What do you have in mind?"

"I think you should get me into Washington, and I should find a way to befriend your old friend John Nicolay. You couldn't do it, but he doesn't know me, and I think I probably can come up with a plan to work my way into his heart."

"That is not happening, Julia. Far too dangerous. I love you more than the world itself, so I am way too selfish to ever agree to put you in harm's way. Nicolay is the President's right-hand man, for crying out loud!"

"Exactly Henry, exactly", Julia looked beseechingly at him. Somehow Henry knew then and there that she would have her way.

The White House, January 6, 1862

What began as a typical grey, cold Monday morning turned into something quite different. As members of Lincoln's cabinet began to file in, the President noticed a tension in the air. He had known his cabinet choices were not only men who wanted his job, but also men who didn't necessarily like each other. He had deliberately chosen for the past several months to ignore the internecine squabbles and to focus on winning the war. It seemed that management style, which some suggested was simply too laisses faire, was going to rear its ugly head on this particular day.

Having welcomed everyone as they assumed their normal seats around the table, the President commented. "It seems something is bothering more than one of you. Perhaps someone could tell me what it is.

Secretary Cameron spoke first. "It seems, Sir, that my fellow secretaries do not approve of the job I am doing. In particular, they think I have been feathering my own nest, and handing out plumb jobs like so much candy. I will not tolerate this attack on my good name, and I am here to resign my post."

Lincoln had heard rumors of Cameron's alleged cronyism, but was unaware the situation had developed to the extent of what appeared to be a junta; not against him, but against one of his chosen secretaries.

"Is this something you gentlemen have decided without my involvement?"

His cabinet looked blankly at him, and then Salmon Chase spoke. "It is Mr. President. We did not want to bother you with a matter that we thought was best to resolve between ourselves."

"And you, Simon. This is actually what you wish?"

"I believe it is in our best interest as a leadership team, Sir, and yes, if this is the way to clear my name, I support the desires of this group."

Lincoln took a few moments to ruminate, took a deep breath, and spoke. "Well, then, I accept your resignation. But you will leave this House with your head held high. I support you, and I thank you for your service. These are not easy times, and the good Lord knows none of us live in such impregnable glass houses that we can afford to cast stones at others." With that he looked disapprovingly at his Cabinet. "I suppose it is best then, that you take your leave."

Everyone stood and there were awkward handshakes around the table. Cameron left the room.

"That was not how I expected this day to start. I suppose since you gentlemen have ambushed me with that bombshell, you also have a plan in store for his replacement? And before you answer, may I remind you again of something I have reiterated since we first met last spring.

America will never be destroyed from the outside. If we falter and lose our freedoms, it will be because we ourselves destroyed them."

Secretary Seward spoke first. "It is the desire of the group, Mr. President, that Edwin Stanton assume the post."

Lincoln looked around the room and saw everyone nodded their approval. "Interestingly, if I had to choose, it would be him. So let us not waste time hand-wringing. He shall assume those duties post haste. In the meantime, can someone here update me on the war?

"Yes Sir," said Seward. "Unfortunately, my report is short, as it is not my primary brief. There has been very little progress. As you know, General McClellan is not well, so little has occurred." (Lincoln had been informed that McClellan was under the weather.) "I can report, however, that we have assembled some eighty ships and over 10,000 men to impose our naval blockade on the Carolinas. I do believe we are succeeding in cutting off the rebel efforts to both import and export goods."

"That is good news, indeed." said Lincoln, "But where are the plans to proceed on the ground? Why on earth is nothing being done?"

Seward replied, "Sir, General McClellan continues to insist we are not ready for a major campaign into the south, and no opportunity has presented itself."

"Good Lord!" exclaimed Lincoln. "This is endless. Dammit," he said, pounding the table, "if General McClellan is not going to use my army, I would like to borrow it for a while!"

While he was being quite serious, it was a funny line, and everyone smiled at the President's humor. Secretary Chase spoke, "We also have some plans in motion in the west. General Halleck has asked General Grant to prepare his men to take Fort Henry on the Tennessee River. If we take Fort Henry, it opens the door to the rest of Tennessee and then Alabama. Grant, it seems, does not suffer from shyness in the face of battle. It will be interesting to see how he fares."

"And what about the rebels?" Lincoln asked.

"Yes, fair enough. Best we can tell, our pressure on their supply lines is making it hard for them to create supply chains. Their men are willing and their spirit is strong. But we have better arms, more ammunition, more supplies, you name it. They have a General who excelled at Bull Run. Thomas Jackson. He was teaching at VMI when war broke out. He is now called 'Stonewall' Jackson, due to his heroics at Manassas. We're told he is gearing up for a campaign in the Shenandoah Valley. He is outnumbered. But we worry, Sir. He carries with him an air of invincibility, and it seems to rub off on his troops."

"When General McClellan is up on his feet again," said the President, his eyes boring into Seward's, "I want his focus on taking Richmond. If we take Richmond, we break the enemy's back, before the enemy makes us take the entire south. The minute he is well again, I want him here, telling us his plans. Are we clear? I assume Mr. Stanton will be here post haste and this will all be conveyed to him."

"We will swear him in as soon as possible, and your instructions are as clear as the sky is blue, Sir."

"It's snowing outside, Secretary Seward."

"Ahh, just an expression Mr. President. I think you have spoken with clarity. We understand your wishes."

As bad as the cabinet meeting was on that January 6 day, little did any of those men know just how horrible things would be 159 years later, when the capital building was stormed by angry Americans who had been led to believe their candidate for President had been wrongfully declared the loser. That January 6 event would make the trials and tribulations of Lincoln's cabinet meeting pale in comparison.

The President's early Cabinet, featuring Secretaries Welles, Seward, Blair, Cameron, Chase, Bates, and Stanton.

(Edwin Stanton replaced Simon Cameron as Secretary of War, and he is looking over Cameron's shoulder in this depiction.)

CHAPTER EIGHT
NEW YEAR-SAME OLD, SAME OLD

As it happened, McClellan did recover from his flu-like symptoms, and was consequently summoned to the White House on January 12th. The full cabinet was present, and the meeting took place upstairs in Lincoln's office. It was yet another cold, grey winter day.

The General took his seat, hand stuffed in his tunic. Lincoln silently marveled at the man's Napoleonic complex. Lincoln had it on very good advice that McClellan had referred to him as a gorilla, or baboon, or some monkey-like reference. The man's ego and lack of manners were quite extraordinary. "I understand you continue to be impatient for a battle plan, Mr. President."

Lincoln looked at him and shook his head. "I want one thing, General. I want a leader who will take advantage of our overwhelming superiority on all fronts, develop a battle plan, execute it, and end this horror show. I continue to ask myself whether you are that man, as you have shown me no reason to believe you are. Did I make a mistake appointing you?"

McClellan's face reflected the level of umbrage he took at such a perceived affront. He looked around the table to see if he had the implicit support of any cabinet members. Their faces told him he was rather alone. Not even his friend, Secretary of War Stanton, threw him a lifeline. "Mon Dieu", he began, "what little faith! I come to tell you I anticipate making a move to take Richmond. It will be soon. Before the Ides of March, we could well be in Richmond itself." He sat back, looking smugly around the table.

"I'm pleased to hear that, General" the President responded. "Pray tell us the plan."

"Mr. President, I am sorry, but I cannot do that. I do not trust anyone. I am your Supreme Commander. You must trust that I will get this done. You are, Sir, with all due respect, in over your head. It is best to leave these military matters to a military man."

One could have heard a pin drop, not just in that office, but perhaps in the entire house. Lincoln was a man who was not riled easily. Those who had now worked with him for nearly a year knew he stayed level-headed no matter what the challenge at hand. He looked at the General, and calmly said, "General, I'm sure you will go home to your nice house and reconsider the ill choice of words we just heard. And in no more than a week's time, you can come back here to provide the detail we just requested." He stood and left the room.

Retreating to the living quarters, he ran into Mary, who was quietly darning those socks that never seemed to stay in one piece. "Abraham, you look perturbed."

"Mary, you wouldn't believe me if I told you. I'm going for a walk."

John Nicolay was doing exactly the same thing. He had not been taking notes for the cabinet meeting, and needed to catch some of the cold, brisk air to help shake the cobwebs created by endless paperwork he processed on behalf of his boss. He turned a corner on 15th and Constitution Avenue and abruptly bumped into the most beautiful girl he had ever seen in his life. She yelped in surprise and backed off. "Oh, I am so sorry," he said, his face growing flusher by the second.

"Well, that is not a normal way to meet a woman on the street," she said laughing.

Her laugh, her eyes; he was smitten. He had never really even noticed anyone since that horrible experience back in college. Always too busy working; maybe he had just been making himself too occupied to think about women.

"I wasn't paying attention. I truly do apologize. I hope you are not hurt?"

"Oh, you didn't hurt me. My goodness, a young lady needs to be tougher than that these days."

Nicolay didn't know what to say. And for a young man who usually knew exactly what to say, he was stupefied. "Well, then, good. I will take my leave." He bowed slightly and began to step aside.

"Oh, a proper gentleman would invite a lady some place for a cup of tea. It is that time of day, don't you know?"

Nicolay wasn't sure if he was dreaming. The most beautiful woman in the world just asked him to have a cup of tea. This kind of thing just didn't happen. "Why, yes, errrrr, of course, you are right. That is exactly what I should have done. I happen to know a tea house on 17th. Why don't we go have a cup?"

"My name is Lora. Lora Withering." She put her hand out.

"Yes, well, I am John Nicolay. It is a pleasure to make your acquaintance."

The White House,
January 27th, 1862

Much had happened in the two weeks since Lincoln threw down the gauntlet with his top General. Then again, another way to look at the situation was that not much at all had occurred. McClellan had not come back to the White House; thus leaving Lincoln and his cabinet just as much in the dark as to how the General planned to take

Richmond as they were on the 12th of January.

Lincoln had not been idle. He also had some very good information about rebel troop strength outside the capital, again near Manassas, and Centerville, and north of the Rappahannock River. Enemy troop strength had been provided by Allan Pinkerton; the man who had first advised Lincoln of the plot on his life when he was travelling to the capital for his swearing-in ceremony. Pinkerton was presently in McClellan's employ. And while the numbers of troops he indicated were still massed within thirty miles of the capital, Lincoln looked for ways to capitalize while his General seemed to be paralyzed by the same information.

Perhaps more interesting was the information his aide, John Nicolay had given him. It was information Lincoln made sure was immediately handed to General McClellan. It seemed Nicolay had befriended a young lady whose sentiments lay with the north, but whose father had thrown his lot in with the south. She told Nicolay General Johnston was planning an assault on the Capital (again) and he was massing troops to accomplish the task.

Lincoln was not prepared for a non-committal response from General McClellan on this day, and that is exactly what he got. The General was standing fast with his contention that he and he alone should know the Union army plans for victory. The President listened and then, with his usual alacrity (albeit alacrity with a slightly sharper edge) he said, "General, who is the ranking military officer in this room?"

McClellan responded, "I am."

"That answer is incorrect. I am your senior officer. So, let us all be clear. I am herewith ordering you to begin military operations within the next three weeks. I further order you to communicate the full details of your plans to me and this cabinet. Is there any possible way we do not understand each other?"

"Oh, I hear as clearly as one can read an incoming telegram, Mr. President. I wish I could put my hand on my heart and tell you I think you know what you are doing. But be that as it may, I shall go determine how to minimize the death and destruction you wish to visit upon our troops." The General stood, contemptuously saluted, and left the White House.

Lincoln was beyond being surprised anymore. He watched the General leave, adjusted the papers lying before him on his desk, and began to focus on the matters of state. Secretary Stanton broke the silence. "Mr. President, does anything ever get under your skin? I mean, I know I was an early advocate for the General, but good heavens, Sir, he is impossible! I have never seen such hubris, and his lack of deference to you is appalling. I just don't know how you remain so calm."

Lincoln put his head back and laughed. "I reckon I don't much see the purpose of lowering myself to his level, Mr. Stanton. He is, as my father used to say, a complete 'horse's ass', and a Napoleonic popinjay to boot!"

The entire cabinet laughed. Secretary Chase said "Well, when you put it that way, I guess it makes it easier to let his behavior slide, like water off a duck's back. But still, our success depends on him actually doing something."

"He has a deadline now, gentlemen." Lincoln responded. "If there is no action, we will find another to take his place, and we will continue to do so until we find someone who is willing to fight." Little did Lincoln know how prophetic he was. For while General Grant was quietly making progress on the western front, and would win many a battle over the ensuing year, it would be one year and two days from this particular cabinet meeting before he actually was asked by Lincoln to assume responsibility for the entire army. During that 367-day interim period, there would be more frustrations for the President. Fighting a war was complicated; fighting one with an arm seemingly always tied behind one's back made it agonizingly so.

The White House,
February 20, 1862

While nothing much had transpired, per the usual, on matters war related, the Lincoln household was in deep despair. With his father and mother by his side, young Willie Lincoln succumbed to Typhoid Fever. He was in the bedroom next to Lincoln's office. The President was inconsolable with grief, outdone only by Mary who was beyond despair. Elizabeth Keckley, Mary's wonderful dressmaker, was present. She and Willy had spent much time together over the past year. She saw Lincoln bury his head in his hands and exclaim ""My poor boy, he was too good for this earth. God has called him home. I know that he is much better off in heaven, but then we loved him so. It is hard, hard to have him die!"

She remembered thinking how hugely unfair it was for this man who seemed to have aged twenty years in the past 365 days to not only have to shoulder the burden of trying to preserve the fragile union, but also to suffer the heartbreak of losing a child. Making matters worse was that Tad lay ill in another bedroom; he too was sick with the Typhoid.

Willie's body was taken to the Green Room downstairs, where it would rest until the funeral service. Robert had to be notified at Harvard, and rushed back to Washington. It is said that Mary was so stricken by the loss of Willie she never set foot again in the Green Room.

Lincoln grieved through the funeral, and then, in an amazing display of intestinal fortitude, rededicated himself to running the country. Fortunately, Tad recovered. His death would have sent Mary into a psychological spiral from which she would never have recovered. As it was, Mary was never quite the same.

Five weeks had transpired since the arrogance in the shape of George McClellan had walked out of Lincoln's cabinet meeting. Perhaps of more interest was the fact that more than a year had transpired since Lincoln had been sworn in as President. One whole year, and nothing seemed to have progressed! The President was agitated. Given his stern orders back on January 27, one would have thought much would have happened to advance the war effort. Alas, a confluence of events had led to more paralysis. It was always something. Before this day was over, though, President Lincoln will have relieved General McClellan of his commander's role, and ask him to focus solely on a Virginia based Peninsula campaign. Once again, he asked the General to focus on the objective of taking Richmond. History seemed to be repeating itself. At least the notion of taking Richmond was a recurring theme! While waiting for Secretary Stanton and General McClellan to appear so Lincoln could give him news of his demotion, the President ruminated on the events of the past month.

Three days after the January 27 cabinet meeting, when Lincoln had yet to hear a peep from the General, he issued more orders detailing how he wanted the General to move on Centerville and Manassas (yes, Manassas again) and take advantage of all the intelligence they had been given about General Johnston's position north of the Rappahannock. McClellan had finally responded (after sending Lincoln a 22 page letter detailing why a precipitous move against the south would be devastating) by allowing that he had a plan; it was called his Urbanna Plan. While it was different from that which the President had been voicing, it was based on strangling General Johnston north of the Rappahannock. Once again, it took a few weeks for any movement to be detected. Lincoln was beside himself.

The only good news during the month of February had come from Tennessee, when on the

16th of the month, General Grant had taken Fort Donaldson from the rebels. It was to be the first of many times when the General refused to discuss terms of surrender with the foe he was on the verge of beating. When the southern commander had offered to meet and discuss terms before surrendering the Fort, Grant sent this message. "No terms except unconditional and immediate surrender can be accepted. I propose to move immediately upon your works."

His nickname since West Point had been U.S. Grant. Now the folklore growing throughout the ranks was that U.S. stood for "Unconditional Surrender". Lincoln was beginning to take notice of this General who was rising from relative obscurity. Lincoln could relate. After all, according to all the high society folk on the east coast, he was just a log splitter from Illinois.

Taking Fort Donaldson was not the only good news in Tennessee. Just before the end of February, Union forces would force the surrender of Nashville. This marked the first time during the war that a major city had capitulated. And just three days earlier, even further south, his army had won a battle at Pea Ridge, in Arkansas.

Ulysses S. Grant

Countering the good news coming in from Tennessee and Arkansas was the borderline disaster that was McClellan's Urbanna plan. Having finally begun to mobilize his forces toward General Johnston, spies reported back that General Johnston was not there! Notwithstanding all the intelligence from sources such as Pinkerton and Nicolay's new lady friend, upon closer inspection, it was reported that Johnston had not been north of the Rappahannock for weeks. He had left behind fake batteries of fallen pines, assembled to look like cannon. It was all a mirage. Once again, the President had been misled. Once again, his top General had failed him. Once again, months had gone by and not one ounce of effort or progress had been made on the plan to take Richmond.

And then, adding injury to insult, the insurrectionists had built an ironclad ship and just two days before, the ship had damaged several Union wooden naval vessels in a battle on the James River in Virginia.

When McClellan did arrive later that day, the first steps would be taken to position the army for new overall leadership. Lincoln would proceed in the meantime with no overall commander.

That did not mean the President was sitting idly by. Indeed, unbeknownst to anyone but Nicolay and Secretary Stanton, on this very day, he was also promoting General Halleck to commander of the army of the Mississippi, thus pulling all forces under one chain of command in the western theater. Generals Grant and Sherman would now be under Halleck's command.

CHAPTER NINE
INEXORABLE STONEWALLING

Richmond, Virginia,
March 17, 1862

The Memmingers were having Stonewall Jackson over for dinner. Henry and Janie would attend, as would President Jefferson Davis. Mary Memminger, the acknowledged ruler of the household, had her staff busy preparing a royal feast. Jackson had quietly become the most celebrated General of the young war. His stoic "Stonewall" heroics at the Battle of Manassas had become the stuff of legend. He was a quiet man. He didn't drink or cuss. But his mind was always churning. All that said, he could sit through a nice dinner without losing his patience, and he knew as well as anyone that being a general meant playing nicely in the social sandbox from time to time.

Dinner was preceded by cocktails on the front porch, looking out on an idyllic block long and wide park across the street from their house. It being March, the cherry trees were in full bloom, and the sun had begun to set in the evening noticeably later in the day. Jackson loved the spring. It was a time for a man to renew his purpose. He knew more than anyone how important that was, as on the very next day, he would be departing again for the Shenandoah Valley, where he would embark on a campaign that tormented the Yankees and President Lincoln for months to come. He had been there in February, but pulled back when General Banks greatly outnumbered his army. Now though, it appeared General Banks was being called to divert troops to General McDowell, whose army was forming part of McClellan's long- awaited move on Richmond.

At this moment however, he sat on the porch taking in the cool evening air and watching the sun disappear on the western horizon, he was as content as he had been for months.

A servant appeared and distributed drinks to the group. Jackson had ordered an iced tea; this was a new non-alcoholic drink fashioned from water with black tea leaves left steeping in same for hours. Once fully saturated, the liquid was poured through a strainer into a pitcher, (a Tiffany crystal one at that-after all, the Yankees had to do something right) and then poured over ice shaved off a block. Ice was also a new thing, and quite the rage in Richmond. It was also getting harder and harder to find, as all the components of the apparatus needed to make ice came from northern manufacturers. Needless to say, parts were in short supply. The coup de grace for this new refreshing drink was something Jackson claimed as his own invention. Borrowing from the British, he added lemon, and then, a uniquely southern addition; mint. He knew the Londoners would be horrified at the notion of adding ice to tea, but then again, they were horrified eighty years before, when the colonies revolted against their staid ways. "Life goes on", he chuckled to himself as he sipped his tea.

The rest of the group enjoyed some Kentucky bourbon, but Julia Frank drank it as part of a mint julep, a particularly popular drink throughout the southern states.

Henry was enjoying himself, listening to his father, President Davis, and General Jackson talk about everything and nothing at the same time. It seemed the evening, not necessarily by design, was one where everyone present was letting off a little steam. Lord knows they were due some reprieve from the pressures of disengaging from the union. While listening, he couldn't help but stare at the love of his life. What a girl! She was sitting next to Jackson, and engaging him with thoughtful conversation. She was completely comfortable in her own skin. In fact, rather than wearing a traditional dress of the time, she wore a plain white shirt and black pants, with leather boots. It was quite unusual, but Henry thought she looked beautiful, and admired her for her individuality.

There was a lull in the conversation which lasted only momentarily. Jeff Davis looked at Janie and said, "I understand, young lady, that you actually volunteered to infiltrate Washington and befriend Mr. Lincoln's aide, John Nicolay?" His tone of voice rose thus leaving the inference that he was opening the door for her to respond.

Janie answered, "Yes Sir. It just seemed like something I should do for the cause. Truthfully, he was a very nice man, and I felt a tinge of remorse for lying to him." Davis frowned, and Janie immediately noticed, put her head back, and laughed. "Just a tinge, Mr. President. My loyalties are not suspect!"

It was everyone else's turn to laugh. President Davis slapped his knee and responded, "Isn't that the truth. Good heavens. You are a hero. You and Henry have served your Confederacy with distinction! Just think, it has been more than a year since these troubles were begun, and Mr. Lincoln and his Generals have not been able to do a darn thing. The misinformation we have managed to continue to feed the northern beast has played a large role in this incredible outcome." He lifted his bourbon. "To you both. If we had hundreds of Janie Franks and Henry Memmingers, this war would already be over!"

Davis shifted his gaze to General Jackson. "So General, I believe you are leaving town tomorrow?"

"Yes Sir", Jackson responded while scratching his scraggly beard. "I am off west again to the Shenandoah Valley. I plan to outrun and outgun the Yanks at every turn. The boys are looking forward to it."

"Perfect", Davis said. "You are probably aware the Yanks are presently loading onto ships and moving toward a Peninsula campaign. And we hear McDowell is coming out of hibernation to approach us from the north, while McClellan thinks he is sneaking up on us from the south. I guess since they couldn't muster the energy to take Richmond coming south from Washington, they figure they can surround us. Well, in any event, the more you keep them running in the Shenandoah, the less their chances of success will be right here in Virginee.'"

"Sir", said Jackson, "To be honest, if y'all can keep our boys fed and armed, we will win this war." He looked stern. He was serious. He believed every word he had just spoken. "I'm told that President Lincoln is a student of history. I am a professor of it. Not to mention a student of historical warfare. Sun Tzu, millennia ago, wrote words I took to heart years ago. He said 'All warfare is based on deception. Hence, when we are able to attack, we must seem unable; when using our forces, we must appear inactive; when we are near, we must make the enemy believe we are far away; when far away, we must make him believe we are near' And that, President Davis, is exactly what I will be attempting to do in the Shenandoah." Jackson would have been amused had he known that President Lincoln was also a reader of Sun Tzu.

Chris Memminger spoke up. "General, we are doing our best. I implore you to take that as a fact. You keep doing what you do so well, and we will do our utmost to keep your men fed and armed." Jackson smiled and nodded.

Davis nodded affirmatively and spoke again. "General, you will no doubt be aware that I have asked General Lee to spend time here in Richmond with me and help me strategize. I have said it before, and I will say it again. We have the better generals in this war. You sir, are one of them. Godspeed in the months to come. And let's not forget General Johnston says we have some 60,000 men in the area to protect Richmond. I don't care how many boys the yanks throw at us. We just plumb fight better!"

Mary Memminger interjected. "Yes, indeed Jeff. Well said. And on that note, gentlemen, and Janie, its supper time. Let's start taking care of our troops by making sure General Jackson leaves Richmond on a full stomach, shall we?" She did not need to twist any arms. Everyone stood and moseyed into the dining room.

Robert E. Lee

The Soldier's Home,
March 17, 1862

The Soldier's Home sits on a hill about four miles north of the White House. President Lincoln had visited it once in 1861, and viewed a cottage on the premises. He determined that for the rest of his years in office, his "summer White House" would be in that cottage. On this fine spring day, however, he took a ride out to the cottage. Accompanying him was Kate Chase. Mary was on another shopping trip in New York City.

Lincoln and Kate's friendship had provided much solace to the President. She was smart, thoughtful, and had proven to be a very good sounding board. Lincoln had no regrets that he had agreed to have Kate serve as an advisor for Women's Affairs. While women could not vote, Lincoln reckoned they still needed a voice, and he could think of no better role for Kate Chase. She had not let him down.

Lincoln's security team had grown. Accompanying the carriage out to the cottage were thirty mounted soldiers; fifteen on each side. As they left the city, they noticed a young boy, who couldn't have been more than five years old, standing rigidly and saluting the President as they rode by. Lincoln stood in his carriage and saluted back.

"What a great country." He said. "That boy back there is why we must win this conflict. We must keep this dream alive, Kate."

"Oh I know, Abraham. So, along those lines, I have a question, if I may?" She looked at him and he nodded in such a way as for her to infer that of course she could ask anything she wished. "It's about the slaves. I know you have said repeatedly this war is not about slavery. It first and foremost is about preserving the Union. I get it. But the longer this goes on, is there actually any way to do that and yet have slavery continue?" She looked imploringly at him.

The President looked at her and then stared ahead. "A vexing question, my friend. A vexing question indeed. How is it that you are the one to ask the right questions!" It was more of a statement than a question. "Pierce and Buchannan were stymied by it. In the end, their presidencies will likely be lost in the dustbin of history because of this horrible situation. They could never achieve consensus. Pierce tried to favor the right of states to choose, and he leaned on the Constitution as his rationale. Of course, as written, he was dead right. But his being dead right pretty much did him in and made him a one term President. And Buchannan fared no better. So yes, dear Kate, you are right. There can be no outcome for this horrible war that does

146

not involve the end of slavery."

Kate listened intently. "But if that is the case, then why not end it now?"

"Kate, this is between us. Your father doesn't even know. But this summer, I will draft a proclamation freeing all slaves. And I will keep it in my desk drawer until such time that I think its issuance will have the best possible desired effect. Now is not that time." The carriage hit a huge pothole and Kate ended up virtually in Lincoln's lap. She laughed and sat back up on her side of the black leather bench seat.

"Sorry Sir", said the private driving the carriage. "Didn't see that one!"

"That's quite alright, son," Lincoln responded in a warm tone.

Kate was not finished. "But why on earth is now not the time?" She inquired.

"Because we need to be winning. And we are not. We need to have planted seeds of doubt throughout the south; seeds so strong that even the most ardent supporters of the rebellion are doubting the possibility of winning. Then, and only then, would it make sense to free them."

"But these are human beings. You are treating them like pawns in some macabre chess game." Kate exclaimed.

Lincoln looked at her, to see if there was disdain written on her expression. There wasn't. There was just compassion. "Kate, I know this is hard. And I know in my heart slavery is wrong. But slavery has been a reality in the world since Adam and Eve. I suspect centuries from now, there will still be examples of people being suppressed by others. It is a reflection of man's lesser, darker side. I have but one goal. You know what it is. And if in preserving this marvelous Republic, this union of states, I also can end slavery, then I will do so. But I must do so strategically. I can never lose sight of the ultimate aim. In this case, abolishing slavery is not the end, but one of the means toward achieving the end."

Lincoln looked ahead, deep in thought. "You see, Kate, this idea of making preservation of the union my focus, well, it doesn't originate with me. You should read President Washington's farewell address to the American people. When he left office in 1796, he wrote a beautiful letter to all of us. It should be required reading. And he made it very clear that this Union of ours is what binds north with south, and east with west. It is our glue. And I will do everything in my power to see this current tear in the fabric of our union repaired, and that we emerge stronger than ever."

Kate looked thoughtful as she absorbed Lincoln's words. Nothing he said was simple. He was simply not a simple man. They sat silently for the next couple minutes as the mounted guard and carriage approached what would soon become known as Lincoln's cottage.

The carriage came to a halt, and as they were disembarking, she grabbed his hand. The President almost pulled away, but didn't. Looking him in the eyes, she said, "They underestimate you, Abe Lincoln. You are a good man. Don't let them get under your skin. I know your heart is in the right place."

He smiled, and squeezed her hand back. "Thank you. You don't know how much that means to me." As they climbed down from the carriage, Lincoln marveled at what a fine young lady she was, and how lucky some man would be to someday call her his wife.

Walking into the cottage, she said, "Now, let's talk about how we are going to get women the right to vote! That is my job, isn't it?"

Lincoln laughed, and responded. "I had no doubt that subject would eventually surface. All good things in time, Kate. All good things in time."

The Shenandoah Valley,
April 25, 1862

In the five weeks that transpired since General Jackson's dinner in Richmond, he conducted a textbook game of cat and mouse with the Union army. Initially, just a week after he left Richmond, he took his troops up to the northern part of the Valley to what he had been told was a diminished force under the command of General Banks. Well, it is true that the General had diverted some troops to support McDowell's pincer move on Richmond. But what Jackson did not know is that he would be attacking a force still three times larger than his.

The net result in that last week of March was to go down in history as the only time Stonewall Jackson ever lost a battle in the Civil War. More importantly, the battle itself is lost in the fog because his actions over the ensuing month could well have saved Richmond. General Banks chased him down the Valley but could never catch him.

By keeping Banks engaged in the Shenandoah, and by the planting of false information regarding Jackson's intentions to sneak north up the valley and east into Washington, Lincoln felt he had no choice but to not only keep Banks out west. He also ordered McDowell to stop his advance on Richmond, and stay close enough to Washington to protect it should an assault occur. General McClellan's Peninsular Campaign strategy had fallen apart. And it came apart partially because of a letter.

Richmond, Virginia,
April 25, 1862

Janie sealed the envelope with Henry standing by her side. Using her nom de guerre, she had penned a letter to her new "boyfriend", John Nicolay. In it, she apologized for being a "phantom" but she had a family illness which needed her attention, and she was presently in

Illinois. She did not know when she would be back in Washington, but she did want Nicolay to know what she had learned from her southern sympathizing father. Namely, it was that General Jackson had been ordered to sweep up the Shenandoah Valley, and once above Washington, to move with stealth on the nation's Capital.

The rest of the letter contained all the polite formalities as would have been appropriate for a mid-nineteenth century budding relationship. Julia stood and handed the addressed envelope to Henry. He looked at her, hugged her, and said "You are simply amazing. Now I have to get this to our runner. They are postmarking nearly all letters in the north, and this one needs to start in Illinois!" While seemingly a world away, the letter would be in Illinois within thirty-six hours. The Confederacy had connections everywhere. They had the ability to work with a network of riders. The letter with the very misleading information would be received by John Nicolay within seven days.

The Cottage at the Soldiers' Home, May 1, 1862

Lincoln had summoned the cabinet to the Soldier's home for an update and review of matters military, social, and economic. There were reports of social unrest in some of the northern cities. It seemed the well-to-do were buying their way out of being conscripted by the army, and as such, most draftees were comprised on new immigrants to the country. The Irish, in particular, were aggrieved about the seeming injustice inherent in the process. There had been some bloodshed.

Lincoln spoke about the tension. "It is, of course, wrong. Alas, we live in an imperfect world. What I will not accept is a breakdown in law and order. Indeed, adherence to the law is one of the cornerstones that keeps our noble experiment alive." He reached on to his summer desk and picked up a single parchment, on which were handwritten some words. "I would like this released to the press." Looking at

Attorney General Bates, he said, "You know all the right people in the northern media. I'll look to you to get this published."

Bates nodded in such a way that it was clear he was expecting Lincoln to read the document. The President obliged him. "Here is what I have written. 'Let every American, every lover of liberty, every well-wisher to his posterity, swear by the blood of the Revolution, never to violate in the least particular, the laws of the country; and never to tolerate their violation by others. As the patriots of seventy-six did to the support of the Declaration of Independence, so to the support of the Constitution and Laws, let every American pledge his life, his property, and his sacred honor; let every man remember that to violate the law, is to trample on the blood of his father, and to tear the character of his own, and his children's liberty. Let reverence for the laws, be breathed by every American mother, to the lisping babe, that prattles on her lap-let it be taught in schools, in seminaries, and in colleges; let it be written in Primers, spelling books, and in Almanacs; let it be preached from the pulpit, proclaimed in legislative halls, and enforced in courts of justice.'" Lincoln paused and looked up.

"Bravo", Mr. President, "It is with honor and privilege that I will see these words published across the land. No words have been more truly written. Law and order are essential, even if it means we must occasionally strike down one of our own." AG Bates meant every word he said.

"Do you think our country will ever come to a place in history where its leaders do not understand the correlation between love of country, Constitution, and the need to uphold the law and maintain order?" The President asked. His entire cabinet guffawed. Secretary Stanton, through his chuckling, said "Mr. President, let us hope not. For it will be a sad day in America if that ever happens."

"Well then, on to the economy. What is there to report, Mr. Chase?" Lincoln looked enquiringly at the Treasury Secretary.

"We are stretched, Mr. President, but nowhere near any breaking point. My team and I honestly believe, that God forbid this war lasts another 2-3 years, we will be ok. The surviving Union will have debt, but not insurmountable debt."

"Well now," said Lincoln, "This is concise. Well done. Brevity is a virtue from time to time, is it not?" He laughed. "I do have a question though. Let's just say, for instance, that our debt exceeds our national economic output. Is there a time, per se, when a nation's currency is devalued because its lenders run scared and do not think the debt will be repaid?"

Secretary Chase looked at the President. "Very good question, Sir. And the answer, again, in a word, is 'yes'. But I do not think that will be an issue with us. We call what you referred to as 'economic output' our Gross Domestic Product. We call it GDP. And with this war, we are actually increasing our output. That, I guess, is one of the more ironic byproducts of war. Even though we are still, well, certainly in the eyes of Europe, a fledgling nation, our Treasury is growing and it won't be long before our GDP exceeds some European countries." He paused and looked at Lincoln. The President motioned with his hand that he should continue. "So, to answer your question, my biggest fear is not whether our creditors will run away from lending money to the United States. Nor do I worry about our ability to pay off our debt. My worry," Chase looked around the room, "is whether we get to a point at some point long after we are gone, where we are so big and so powerful that we think we can just print money and it will solve whatever challenges may be facing the nation at that time. That, gentlemen, may sound absurd, but believe me, there will come a day when we outgrow the supply of gold as our safety net. And when that day comes, we will be printing and borrowing money backed by one thing. Do you know what it is?" He looked around the room again, and could tell they were all stumped. "The word is 'faith.'" The President eyed him somewhat circumspectly.

"Faith?" Said the President.

"Yes Sir. In the absence of gold, of which some day there simply won't be enough to provide the safety net for any national currency, the only thing that will keep currencies afloat is the faith in the country whose Treasury Department is printing the money. And God forbid if the leaders of our country, when and if that happens, don't take their sacred oaths to defend and protect the Constitution to heart. As I say, when this challenge does happen here, we will be long gone. Let us pray the men in the room at that time have enough fiber to manage through."

"Well then", said Lincoln, "I wish I hadn't asked the question!" Once again, the President had broken the ice, and his Cabinet laughed genuine laughs. "But you know", he continued, looking at the entire group, "I have enlisted Secretary Chase's daughter to advise me on women's affairs, and after listening to her, I would find fault in something you just said."

"Oh?" responded Chase, "What has my daughter done!"

"Well, you said that someday '...the men in the room' will have to sort out the problems of the day. According to your daughter, when the day that you describe arrives, it will be the men and women in that room!" Everyone laughed again, this time uproariously. Chase, one could see, was just shaking his head about his headstrong daughter. Lincoln concluded the conversation with this. "I must say, Gentlemen, I wouldn't sell Miss Chase short. I suspect, no matter how far-fetched that seems, she is probably spot-on. Now, let's move to Secretary Stanton and the war. Please tell me something good!"

Stanton cleared his throat. "I wish I could do that, Sir. As you know, we are stalled at Yorktown. McClellan stands by his decision to lay siege two and half weeks ago, rather than a frontal attack. I disagree with his position. We have it on good word that he outnumbers General John Magruder's troops by four to one, has more cannon, arms, you name it. It seems like Manassas all over again. In fact, he has expressed dismay that General McDowell has stayed put between us and Richmond to protect the Capital."

"He has four times as many men, and yet he didn't attack?"

"Yes. That is correct. We have it on good advices that Magruder and the others under General Johnston are quietly pulling back toward Williamsburg and trying to form a defense around Richmond. It appears General McClellan is considering a measured pursuit."

Lincoln looked as though he may be ill. "What else on other fronts?"

"Ah, well we have better news. General Grant has won a battle of attrition at Shiloh. It was a messy affair, Mr. President. Tens of thousands of casualties. It seems General Grant is earning his nickname."

Lincoln's eyebrows went up. "Remind me what that is?"

"Well, his nickname coming out of West Point was U. S. Grant. The scuttlebutt around the army camps is that Grant only knows one direction; forward. And he is willing to pay the price for moving forward with blood and bones. He is not interested in negotiating terms of surrender. Thus, the U. S. is now thought to mean "Unconditional Surrender.""

Lincoln smiled. "This may sound cavalier, or even a little crass, but it sounds to me like we need a few more U. S. Grants in this army!"

"On other fronts, we took Fort Pulaski, a rebel fort protecting the waterway entrance to Savannah, and I am told that Admiral Farragut is days away from taking New Orleans and controlling the mouth of the Mississippi." Lincoln nodded appreciatively. "Lastly, I am told our month-long siege of Fort Macon, the one that protects Beaufort, will likely fall in the next couple days. In short, Mr. President, we are doing fine in the south. It is only here, a heartbeat away from the

Capital, that we seem to be stuck in quicksand."

Lincoln came as close to fuming as he was capable. "It's infuriating. I mean, I am pleased we are making progress in the south. But that is the long game. The end of this mess lies a few miles down the road. Richmond! Why are we paralyzed? It is truly amazing. Does it not seem that at every turn, the enemy is simply better informed and better prepared? Why is that?"

At that moment, there was a knock on the door, and John Nicolay walked in. The mud on his pants led the Cabinet to all conclude he had ridden out to the Soldiers' Home from the White House, and his horse hadn't been spared.

"John, good to see you, although surprising to see you", Lincoln spoke. "Please have a seat and tell us why you have ridden out."

Nicolay wasted no time grabbing a chair and joining Lincoln and his team. All the cabinet members by this time knew him well, and had figured out that he was basically an extension of the President. Not much got to or through the President without John Nicolay being involved and aware. He was young, but very well liked.

He was about to talk when he saw Lincoln looking at him in an awkward way. "Sir, is something wrong?" he asked.

"Oh, sorry John. It's just that you have a piece of mud stuck right in the middle of your chin. It must have kicked up from your ride out. And, well, I'm sure you are about to say something serious, but I am thinking it will be hard to take you seriously as long as that mud is stuck to your face." There was laughter around the room. Lincoln was in one of his moods. He looked at Secretaries Bates and Welles, both of whom had bushy white beards, and said, "Just think if these two had ridden out here. They could be hiding a field of mud in those beards, and no one would be the wiser!"

"Now just a minute, Mr. President," Navy Secretary Welles

responded. "I resemble that remark!"

"Ha! Yes, you do Sir." Lincoln laughed

During this banter, Nicolay had managed to remove the mud from his chin. When the laughter subsided, Nicolay removed a letter from the breast pocket on the inside right of his jacket. "Sir, you will recall I made the acquaintance several weeks ago of a lady of whom I am fond." Lincoln nodded. "She has written me from Illinois, and told me she has it on very good word that General Jackson is positioning his troops in the Shenandoah to make a move from the northwest on toward Washington."

Secretary Stanton spoke up. "John, this is most unusual. You know full well that we hear rumors every day. Why is this any different?"

"Her source is her father, Mr. Secretary, and he is sympathetic to the southern cause. He is actually friends with Jeff Davis. As loyal as he is to the rebels, he is indiscreet when around his daughter. I trust her. I wouldn't be here if I thought for a second I was wasting your time."

Lincoln leaned back in his chair. It creaked. "So the new hero, Stonewall Jackson, who is already giving us fits up and down that damn valley is going to march right into Washington, heh?" Nicolay nodded yes. "Well, aren't we fortunate to have kept General McDowell nearby? Secretary Stanton, will you please make sure McDowell is aware of this news, and obviously alert General Banks out in the Shenandoah. From what I hear, all he is doing is chasing the ghost of Jackson. Now you see him. Now you don't."

Stanton cleared his throat and spoke. "Naturally I will comply, Mr. President. I just want to make sure we are all clear regarding General McClellan in Yorktown. He is hoping we will send McDowell's troops to reinforce his siege and help him advance on Richmond."

Lincoln paused, and then responded. "General McClellan has proven quite capable of accomplishing absolutely nothing! He already

156

outnumbers the enemy and yet sits there laying siege when he should already be knocking on Richmond's door. Now that we know about Jackson's plans, we know for certain we need McDowell here. So, no, we will not send more troops to our sieging General. Tell him to do his damn job!"

Richmond, Virginia, May 15, 1862

"What news today, General Lee?" President Davis was sitting at his desk, accompanied by Secretary Memminger, Robert E. Lee, and Secretary of the Navy, Stephen Mallory.

General Lee sat ramrod straight in his chair. He had a kind face, albeit one that was already becoming permanently creased with the worries of the time. "Well, Sir, I think I may defer to Mr. Mallory for our first piece of news."

Secretary Mallory looked pained. "Hmmph." He looked at Lee. "There are certain times one would prefer to remain out of the spotlight. This, Sir, is one of them." He looked at Jeff Davis and continued. "It seems that yesterday, a small group of slaves managed to board and simply sail our steamship 'Planter' out of Charleston Bay and deliver it to the Yankee army. The officers and crew were apparently enjoying themselves onshore, and the vessel was not guarded."

Davis screwed his face up as if to say "How in the hell could that happen?"

Mallory beat him to the punch. "I know, Sir. It is highly irregular and cannot happen again. We will ensure that it does not. I'm afraid, though, the news is worse. Not only did we lose the ship, but there were four brand new cannon on board. They were destined for our protection of Richmond."

"Good Lord," exclaimed Davis, "We have churches throughout the south donating their bells to us so we can melt them down to make cannon, and we just hand four big guns to the enemy? Why, that is negligence in the extreme. It's not my job to tell you what to do Stephen, but those officers need to suffer some form of reprimand. That behavior cannot be countenanced."

"I quite agree Sir. I will see to it."

Davis paused the conversation, got up, and poured himself a glass of water. "Let's look at the bright side of things, shall we? Yes, we are already constrained by lack of men, arms, and food. But we knew that would happen, didn't we? What do we have that they don't? We have the will to win, the Generals who know how to win, and perhaps most importantly, we have guile!"

Memminger smiled. Lee smiled. Mallory was a little slower on the uptake. "Guile, Mr. President?"

"Oh yes. Guile. First we had General Scott onside. Unfortunately, the Yanks finally figured out he was just slightly past his prime. Then, of course, we have General McDowell, who very nicely delayed events leading up to the Manassas victory. And even now, the Yanks are holding him back to secure the Capital. We know for certain he is in no hurry to do anything.

And then, as though the Gods haven't already looked down favorably upon us, Lincoln put that egomaniac McClellan in charge of his Potomac troops. He might as well be one of ours, for as good as he has done on the Union front!"

Looking at Chris Memminger, Davis went on to say, "And you may not know all the details, but Chris's son and girlfriend have been instrumental in planting seeds of disinformation within the White House. Lincoln doesn't know whether he is coming or going. He must be mighty frustrated. Right now, he is holding McDowell back from advancing on Richmond, because he thinks Jackson is making a move on Washington. Jackson is running up and down the Shenandoah Valley, winning skirmishes and making himself scarce. He's driving the Yanks nuts! And even Stonewall has himself his own femme fatale; a young Virginia lass, from the western parts, who seems to do very well with the Yankee officers. Stonewall tells General Lee she is a very good source for the Yanks' troop locations…great name for a spy too. Belle Boyd.

Anyway, best I can tell, we just need to be prepared for McClellan, when and if he ever does get off his ass and moves up to Richmond from his southern position. I have no doubts at all that we will defend this city. Little Napoleon doesn't have an ounce of guile in him!"

General Lee smiled. "Well, I think you have covered the military update. There is one good piece of news out of Charlotte. We have 1500 men now working in a new foundry. They are making various types of munitions, and they tell me they have an engineer who has finally figured out how to make a perfectly round cannonball. Even the Yanks haven't mastered that one!

As for McClellan, well, while I don't disagree that he has been anything but a laggard, we need to recognize that General Johnston is slowly but surely retreating back up north here toward Richmond. And while the Yanks are moving like snails, they are indeed moving toward us. About half of them are across the Chicahominy River now, and there isn't much standing between them and us except General Johnston! At some point soon, there's gonna be a brawl, and we sure 'nuff need to win it.

I'm not sure I have much more to add. All I can really say is," he looked at Memminger, "I hope you can find some money for us so we can feed and equip our boys. You know, soldiers can only fight so long on empty stomachs."

"We hear you General. Believe me. We do." Memminger spoke with a solemn tone.

Seven Pines Village, Virginia,
June 2, 1862

Much had transpired since Jeff Davis had met with General Lee two weeks before, and much of what General Lee told him near the end of that meeting had come true. On May 31, General Johnston had indeed taken advantage of the Union army's having been cut in half by the Chicahominy River, and had attacked them on the south side of it. Neither side performed particularly well. President Davis had travelled down the Peninsula to witness events first hand. In truth, the fight last some three days, and was a stand-off. That did not, however, stop General McClellan from telegraphing D.C. and bragging of his army's strong showing.

General Johnston suffered a chest wound, and his war effort was over. On June 1st, President Davis gave Robert Lee command over his army. This would prove to be yet another thorn in President Lincoln's side. Lee moved from advisor status to field commander, and the rebels had yet another potent weapon at their disposal.

The Seven Days Battles, Virginia,
June 25–July 1, 1862

It took Robert E Lee a little less than a month to prepare his forces for the first major effort under his supreme command. General McClellan was within fifteen miles of Richmond, but hadn't moved since his last battle at Seven Pines. He was insisting on reinforcements, and President Lincoln was not budging. McClellan continued to forget that he was not actually the Commander-in-Chief.

Over the course of seven days, starting June 25th, Lee won battle after battle. It is true that he lost more men than did McClellan. But there was a reason. The rebel forces were constantly the aggressors. They were pushing McClellan back, and ensuring that he would never march into Richmond. The various battles came to a close when Lee realized he had accomplished his mission, and he pulled back closer to his President and capital city. McClellan's Peninsula Campaign officially ended. He had accomplished nothing. Tens of thousands of American boys were dead.

The President's Cottage, Soldiers' Home, Washington D.C., July 4, 1862

Robert was home for the summer. Mary and Tad were also in situ, and the four remaining Lincoln's were all in the President's Cottage, hoping to escape the trials and tribulations of the Presidency for at least a couple days. July 4th fell on a Friday, so the Lincoln's planned on a calm long weekend.

The President had missed having Robert home. It seemed he had grown into a man, and Lincoln felt as though he had somehow missed the process. It was 5 PM on the 4th, and the two of them sat in rocking chairs on the front porch. A couple military guards were visible, but all in all, it was quiet and almost normal.

"Father", Robert broke the ice, "I don't know how you do it. It has been a horrible year and a half. Yet you remain stoic. Does it weigh you down? I mean, how can it not?"

Abe turned his head to the left and looked kindly at his oldest son. "Yes, of course it does, Robert. But if I don't bear the burden, then who? You know, earlier today, I was re-reading an address I issued to our citizens a year ago on this date. I thought, hmmmm, I couldn't have said it better myself. But then again, I wrote it, so there you go!" They both laughed. "Do you remember it?"

"I do", said Robert. "It was a rather long, but, yes, well-written dissertation on why you had no choice but to protect the Constitution, and the Republic by taking us to war to fight the insurrection."

"Yes, that's the one. I closed with these words. 'And having thus chosen our course, without guile and with pure purpose, let us renew our trust in God and go forward without fear and with manly hearts.' You know, son, as I look back on these several months, there are scant few of us who can put their hands on their hearts and say they have acted without guile. I would like to think I am one of those few."

Robert took a sip of his bourbon, a drink he had learned to enjoy at Harvard. "Do you mean you are ill-served by those around you? Or do you mean you just now are discovering the natural state of man?"

Lincoln rolled his head back and let a laugh out. It felt good. Maybe even a wrinkle or two in his fatigued face disappeared for a moment. "Well, I see you are learning the liberal arts up there at that fancy school. Hah. No, I think I learned of man's general nature years ago. What I mean to say is that I feel this war effort has been stymied at every turn. We have lost the initiative. We could have ended it before it truly began. Now…well, now, I fear we are in it for the long haul. And it is just going to get much worse before it gets any better."

"But why father? Why haven't the Generals moved faster? I mean, I am torn. We have professors at Harvard who argue that we should not have gone to war. They say Presidents are always pugilists; that we should just have let the southern states secede and form their own imperfect union. I mean, in a way, I understand. We would not bankrupt the treasury, and, God forbid, have to raise money through taxation on individual's wealth, which, ummm, can we come back to that, because I hear you are thinking about supporting Secretary Chase's wealth tax…but back to the point, are you sure you are right?"

Lincoln sighed. "Oh, the price of a superior education." Robert sat back as if taking umbrage. "No son, please don't react defensively. Since God was a small child, fathers and sons have had such conversations. And you must know I am immensely proud of you and your intellect. You will, notwithstanding who your father is, do very well in this world. All I ask is that you accept that I have a few more years under my belt." Lincoln subconsciously looked down to make sure he was wearing a belt. He was, so he continued, "I respect you. But let me tell you something about Harvard, or that horrible place in New Haven, Yale. You see, they are full of very smart people. But from my scrappy, horseback riding lawyering days in Illinois, I wish more of them had lived in the real world. Academics are great. They make you think. I just don't think they have a clue about how to manage themselves or their thoughts in a prism of reality. This war, Robert, is real. To let the Union be torn asunder, why, it's just not possible. We cannot let it happen!" Lincoln grew animated and finished his sentence with a hands in the air flourish.

"OK Dad, I see your point. So getting back to where we started, why is nothing happening?"

Lincoln paused, sat back, and clasped his hands behind his head. "Son, if I had a penny for every time I have asked myself that question, I would be a wealthy man. Alas, I don't. I do not know the answer, but I have concluded that there simply have to be spies in our midst. Thus my earlier comment about guile. I trust the men around me. I do. But it is impossible to have been so seemingly paralyzed for this long a period of time without our being compromised on many fronts. I only wish I knew who, why, where, and how."

Robert leaned in and listened hard. He was proud of his father; immensely proud. He had known for years that his dad possessed an amazing intellect, and unlike the education his parents had afforded him, he was largely self-taught. He ached for his father's pain; the war, losing Willie, Mary's distance and constant reckless spending. He wondered how his father endured.

"Dad, I don't know. I mean, I guess, obviously I don't know! I feel

163

horribly for you. I will go back to school in September. Lord knows what more bad news awaits you on the military front this summer. I live in a bubble at Harvard. You are living this day to day. I wish I could offer you something more than moral support."

Lincoln looked fondly at Robert, happy that he was making up for lost years. "Son, this conversation has done me wonders. I don't know what the good Lord has in store for me or our country. I do know that I will commit to preserving this Union until the day I die. And I know I have to determine who is undermining our efforts. You know, I feel like Hamlet. Wait, you are at Harvard. Do you remember what Shakespeare had Hamlet say about spies?"

"Hah! Hallelujah!" Robert nearly yelled his enthusiastic response. "Yes, I just read it this year. And I remember thinking about you! He wrote 'When sorrows come, they come not single spies, but in battalions.'"

"Indeed, Robert, indeed."

At that moment, an elderly man came up to the front porch and saluted the President. He was known by everyone at the Soldiers Home and had lived there for more than twenty years. He had entered his tenth decade of life, and lived long enough to see the formation of the Republic. Nathanial Longshorn was his name. His family had been sheep herders in the English countryside for eons. At the age of two, he was moved to Boston, just in time to take a stray bullet in the leg, fired by a British soldier. In his 30's he had fought for his country in the War of 1812. Following that he had farmed land in Virginia, until such time that he could no longer manage, and at the age of 70, he and his wounded leg moved into the Soldiers Home, where he would spend the rest of his days. No one had anticipated this veteran living into his 90's. He had become something of a legend; one of the last Americans to have been alive when the Declaration of Independence was signed.

President Lincoln stood and saluted back. Robert followed suit and stood next to his father.

"May God Bless you, Mr. President." Longshorn stood ramrod straight.

"At ease, Mr. Longshorn." Lincoln smiled and said "We are blessed as a nation to have men like you. You served with distinction and have seen so much of our history unfold before your very eyes. No sir, I must say, it is I who must insist that God bless you!"

The old veteran dropped his salute and smiled. "You stick to your guns, Abe Lincoln. You are doing the right thing." And with that, he ambled off toward his quarters.

A voice from inside the cottage shot through an open window. "Abe, Robert, dinner time. Enough of that boy talk!"

Abe Lincoln and his son Robert, still standing after their brief encounter with the man who had seen the birth of their nation, turned and went inside for dinner.

CHAPTER TEN
EMANCIPATION

The President's Cottage, Soldiers' Home, Washington D.C.,
July 5-September 30, 1862

To the extent the previous eighteen months had given the President no reprieve from the stresses of leading a country at war, the summer of 1862 would bring no relief. He named Henry Halleck his new commanding General in the middle of July and came close to begging him to take bold, decisive steps to stem the tide of the war; a tide that seemed to almost always favor the enemy.

In the middle of that month, he also established the Medal of Honor, the top award for bravery in armed conflict that survives to this day. Military buffs would also be interested in knowing that in this steamy month of July, the notes to what readers today known as "Taps" were first written and played by bugle in the field of battle. The notes were originally constructed to signal time for the men to extinguish their lights, but soon after spreading through the ranks, the custom of playing Taps at military funerals took hold for perpetuity.

While McClellan's ill-fated Peninsula Campaign petered out, it did not mean the Yankees had pulled out of Virginia. They were still there, and still an existential threat to Richmond. On August 9th, General Halleck had his General Nathaniel Banks take on the rebel troops in what became the battle of Cedar Run. As with most battles throughout the war, the Union had the advantage of more troops, supplies, and munitions. What the Union force did not have, however, was Stonewall Jackson. While the early parts of the battle seemed to favor the north, Jackson rode into battle, rallied his troops and won an impressive victory. Once again, the north retreated with its tail between its legs.

It got worse. Jackson proved to be as elusive as ever. There were rumors of his being somewhere near Manassas, the site of the first Union disaster back in 1861. Halleck dispensed General Pope with his battalion to the area. In reality, General Lee was there, and Jackson had circled back around after his victory at Cedar Run, and captured the supply depot in Manassas. Not surprisingly outnumbered again, the Confederate army was simply better. Generals Longstreet and Jackson, under General Lee routed the Yankee army. General Pope, by all accounts a pompous man, attempted to blame his subordinates for gross dereliction of duty. While he was successful in deflecting some of the blame, he had seen the last of his duties on the eastern front, and was soon relegated to duty further to the west.

In short, it was a horrible summer for the Union cause. If there was a silver lining, it was probably that these victories gave General Lee the false hope that he could take his defensive war and go on the offense. For it was the victory at the Second Battle of Bull Run that emboldened Lee enough to begin formulating a plan to move north and take the battle(s) to Pennsylvania.

The first foray was into Maryland. While there may have been no shortage of southern sympathizers in Maryland, it was officially a Union state. Lee was on the move in September, and while concerned about the concentration of Army of the Potomac troops under none other than George McClellan, (still licking his wounds after the failed Peninsula Campaign) Lee was emboldened when General Jackson grabbed Harper's Ferry from the bluecoats.

Notwithstanding a withering attack on General Longstreet's troops on September 14th, Lee dug in and three days later the bloodiest battle of the war took place. It is remembered as the Battle of Antietam. There are differing accounts of who won. Seen through an objective lens, it is fair to say that neither side won the battle, but the Union lost the war of opinion. All may best be explained back at the White

House.

The White House, Washington, D.C.
September 21, 1862

President Lincoln sat with his cabinet. It was 10 AM on a Sunday morning. The days blurred together. No one on the cabinet was complaining. It would be one thing if the President was lollygagging his way through the week. That was hardly the case. He worked all day, every day. So when he convened a Sunday meeting, it neither surprised nor angered his cabinet. It is worth mentioning that this "Team of Rivals", as his cabinet would be labeled more than a century later by historian Doris Kearns Goodwin, had grown to respect their boss. They had watched him bear the burden of a nation torn asunder. They had come to see that he was a better version of themselves. He was not a man to be trifled with. He was compassionate, but could be cold as a stone when duty demanded rock solid frigidity.

"Well now," he started, "I apologize if I have impinged upon your plans for church. It is not in my nature to get in the way of the big man upstairs!"

Secretary Stanton beat the others to the punch with a chortle. "No Sir, I think it is safe to say we have all done our share of praying and there isn't a man amongst us who is wondering whether he is listening!"

"Well, you have a point there Edwin." Lincoln looked up at the ceiling, as though he could see straight through to the heavens. "If you do happen to be lending an ear, dear Lord, we could use a hand down here." There was more chortling. "So, gentlemen, back to the situation at hand. We have had our backsides routed at Cedar Run, Bull Run, and just 4 days ago, I think it is safe to say the best possible view of what happened at Antietam is that we didn't lose. But the carnage; my heavens, the reports are horrible."

Lincoln stood up, as he was wont to do when he started talking. His face displayed intensity. It was as though a part of him was somewhere else. He would look at the men around the cabinet table, and seemingly stare through them. "Once again, General McClellan had General Lee outnumbered and outgunned. And despite the standoff on the battlefield, General Lee was smart enough to know that he could not win a protracted battle, so he withdrew. Can anyone here tell me why on earth General McClellan ignored my instructions to pursue General Lee? Why would he let a tired, smaller force retreat to fight another day? I am beside myself."

There was a lot of shuffling around the table. It fell to Edwin Stanton to speak again. "Sir, I do not have an answer that will mollify you. I believe the General thinks Mr. Lee's force is considerably larger than our intelligence says it is. He thinks if he had pursued the Confederates, he would simply have pushed the stalemate into Virginia and lost more lives in the process."

"He must be mad!" Abe Lincoln exclaimed. This man is the living personification of that old expression 'often wrong, but never in doubt'. Secretary Stanton, he's done. We can find the right time to relieve him, but he is finished. He has ignored me repeatedly. He has failed to win any battle of significance. He is an immodest man with, ironically, much about which to be very modest! I've had it with him."

Lincoln didn't even give Stanton a chance to respond. He continued "Now, gentlemen, I have been waiting on a victory to do something important. Our generals seem steadfast in their refusal to actually provide us with one. To hell with it. The first order of the day is that we leave this meeting united in our position that Antietam was a victory! We will tell any and all who will listen that we stopped Bobby Lee in his northern-headed tracks, and sent him running back to Virginia. Now you may wonder why? Well, here's the situation. Several months ago, I wrote a simple paper I've called the

Emancipation Proclamation." At this, heads did turn, and to the extent anyone was going through the motions listening to him, he now had their rapt attention.

"That's right. I am going to free the negroes in all states that joined the Confederacy. Is it a cynical move? Probably. But let's face it. I will give the abolitionists most of what they have been whining about, and it will give the secessionists a hell of a headache on the home front. I have been waiting for some momentum on the battlefield. I can no longer wait. We, gentlemen, are going to use Antietam as the momentum for this announcement, and tomorrow, we are going to announce that any slaves in states now in rebellion are free. Then on January 1ˢᵗ, I will declare a total emancipation. If my generals won't take the battle to the enemy, I darn well will!"

The President stopped pacing, and looked at the men in his cabinet. Then he went back to his chair and sat down.

Attorney General Bates broke the ice. "It's genius. It's nuanced. It's Machiavellian. It's a dagger in their heart. I might, with all due respect, suggest I look over the wording. You know, just to make sure we lawyer it up a little." He smiled.

Lincoln replied, "I wouldn't have it any other way Edward."

Secretary Chase spoke up. "I may be a little behind the billiard ball on this one, so help me out. Why not just declare all slaves free now?"

"Not a stupid question, Mr. Chase." The President smiled as he spoke, which served to severely exaggerate the creases in his face. "You see, I am trying to anticipate my Attorney General's reservations. You will note he has already requested permission to review the statement! In point of fact, freeing all slaves will require a constitutional amendment. I don't have the time or patience for that right now. But since the secessionist states are in rebellion, I can declare their slaves free. So yes, it is nuanced, and yes, it is even perhaps a little Machiavellian. But it removes any legal bickering from the process, at least for now."

"Dangit. I like it. Well done, Sir." Mr. Chase was being genuine in his response.

The meeting lasted another 90 minutes or so. As it drew to a close, the President asked his Secretary of War exactly what General Halleck did with his time. "It seems he is never actually on the battlefield. Is that unfair?"

"Well, no Sir, it is not unfair. The General believes his position is best managed from his office here in the capital. He believes his subordinates should be in the field."

"So I have a clerk leading my army," the President stated. "Eeghads, some of this is rather hard to fathom. Oh well, that will be all, gentlemen."

CHAPTER ELEVEN
MORE BAD NEWS

The Warfront,
October-December, 1862

In Richmond, Jefferson Davis met with his trusted advisors and General Lee. In reality, the spy network had effectively dried up. His main sources of information had either been caught and jailed (if not worse) or simply de-activated. Henry Memminger and Julie Frank were two such cohorts in the latter category. It was simply too dangerous to travel north to the capital. It was this very topic he was discussing.

"General Lee", he said, "I must apologize for the dearth of information my former spy network has been able to supply. We had quite a run for a year and a half or so. Alas, I hope we bought you the time we need."

It was mid-November. October had come and gone with a whimper. There were some skirmishes around the country. On the downside, the North had solidified is grip on control of the Mississippi. This was not an insignificant issue. The Mississippi was the lifeline for the western theater, and all trade ran up and down its coursing waters. Other than that, General Lee had been able to let his troops regain their stamina, after a rugged September.

President Lincoln had finally dispatched George McClellan, and replaced him with Ambrose Burnside. The new leader of the Army of the Potomac had announced a familiar vision; he wanted to move on Richmond.

General Lee cleared his throat and spoke. "President Davis, I could not have asked for more than what you accomplished. I must be honest. Traveler (his faithful horse) and I will go to our graves not knowing whether your machinations or general Yankee incompetence led to our being able to build an army and develop a winning strategy. What I do know is that when this conflagration began, I had no idea how we were going to survive into 1862. The Yanks had all the assets they needed. We were starting from scratch. Why they didn't pounce will remain a mystery forever."

President Davis leaned back in his chair but before he could speak, Secretary of War James Seddon spoke up. (Seddon had just the day before replaced George Randolph as the new man in charge of prosecuting the war. The reader will recall that Judah Benjamin had begrudgingly agreed to assume the role the year before when the original Secretary, Leroy Pope Walker, had been found to have been indiscreet with state secrets.) General, I know you and I are just gettin' to know one another, and yer probably pretty tired of war secretaries. I understand. We haven't really had time to visit. Lemme just say I have the utmost respect for you and how you and your generals have dominated the field of battle. I will not interfere. I am here to help however I can. Ok?"

Robert Lee nodded in assent.

"Good. Now to your question. President Davis is being too humble. There is no question, in my humble opinion, that we sit here today in this amazingly strong position, because of the network of information providers President Davis was able to cobble together. Criminy, he had northern generals working to help us! Yes, the enemy's incompetence has helped immeasurably, but the misinformation and disinformation with which we were able to barrage Lincoln, well, that's why we now enjoy the advantage. Now, what can we do to help you?"

General Lee leaned back in his chair and looked over those sitting around the table. "I thank you for that explanation, Secretary Seddon, and I appreciate your words of support. I'll be brief, which I guess is no surprise. I hear tell the Richmond folk think brevity should be my middle name. I guess I'm not one to dwell on palaver."

Lee reached toward the middle of the table, picked up a crystal pitcher filled with water, and poured himself a glass. "You have heard Burnside wants to focus his troops once again on taking Richmond. Based on their locations, my guess is we are going to have to stop them in Fredericksburg. I can't say when, but it will be before the New Year. My efforts will be focused on planning to send the yanks packing once and for all from this state."

President Davis asked "General, do you ever see this war turning to a point where we take the offensive?"

"Sir", he replied, "I thought for a while before the battle at Antietam that we might be able to muster the troops and energy to move into Pennsylvania. But that battle was too bloody. We suffered unimaginable losses and needed to regroup here in Virginia. The short answer is 'yes'. I want to beat Burnside and then begin to plan for taking the battle to them. I think we can do it. But this," he turned his head to Secretary Seddon, "is where I need your help. We are not adequately fed, clothed, or outfitted. We lack arms and bullets. We need cannons and grapeshot. We have the will, gentlemen, but we need the way."

President Davis coughed and then took the opportunity to respond. "General Lee, I hear you. The Union blockade of our trading ports has been brutal. It's not just your troops. Our people are beginning to lack for basic essentials. We will do our best. But please know we truly are doing all we can to provision your army."

Lee nodded humbly.

The White House, December 25th, 1862

It was, to tell the truth, a rather desultory, melancholy Christmas in the Lincoln household. Mary was still a hollow shell struggling to cope with Willie's death. The other boys and the President did their best to cheer her up, but she wasn't the same and there was an unspoken recognition that she may never return to her former state. Lincoln took some solace in the fact that her depression had slowed her material acquisitions down considerably, but then banished the thought as he realized it was neither the time nor place for such banality.

The President tried hard to focus on his family. It wasn't easy. Just two weeks before the Union army had been pummeled in the Battle of Fredericksburg. Ambrose Burnside had been outmaneuvered by (yet again) a smaller force led by General Lee. For all intents and purposes, the latest effort to move on Richmond had been stymied. It would ensue that Burnside tried to regain momentum in early January, but the effort (which became known as the "Mud March") literally became bogged down and went nowhere.

As Lincoln sat downstairs in the Green Room, he tried to look on contentedly as his family gathered around him. Lost in his own thoughts though, he came to realize that his emancipation of the slaves in the rebellious states was about the only good thing that had happened in months. "Surely", he thought to himself, "this string of horrific outcomes cannot continue forever."

EPILOGUE

The war would drag on for another two and a half years. Its outcome was inevitable. The carnage created whilst the inevitable took place was relentless and ghastly. As mentioned, President Lincoln made Henry Halleck his lead General after relieving George McClellan of his duties. Then, after brief flirtations with the ideas that Generals Burnside, Hooker, Fremont, Meade, or Pope could deliver victory, Lincoln eventually realized that Ulysses S. Grant was the man (along with tough generals such as William Tecumseh Sherman) who would finally turn the tide and win the war of attrition against the south. If Lincoln had lived long enough, he would have resisted the southern expression that lives to this day. Even now, many from south of the Mason-Dixon line refer to the Civil War as the "War of Northern Aggression." Given Lincoln's druthers, it never would have become an all-out assault on the southern states.

The course of the war eventually moved toward an inevitable victory for the bluecoats. General Lee's northern gambit into Pennsylvania was valiant, but ultimately turned the tide against the rebels. Throughout the hot summer days of July 3rd and 4th in 1863, the Battle of Gettysburg was lost as was the city of Vicksburg, Mississippi. The loss of the latter secured control of the Mississippi River for the Union. The loss of the former was the last time the Confederate army was ever in a position to win the war.

Stonewall Jackson died (sadly, by way of friendly fire) two months before, in May of 1863. The outcome of the war became a foregone conclusion, and with Generals such as Grant pushing relentlessly ahead, using the advantages of more men, munitions, and supplies, the outcome was indeed only a matter of time.

While virtually everyone is no doubt aware of President Lincoln's demise in 1865, fewer probably know that the Lincoln family suffered another loss in 1871, when Tad died of tuberculosis at the age of 18.

Robert, however, much as his father had prophesized, did indeed go on to lead a very successful life. He was Secretary of War for President Garfield, and Minister of the Court of St. James for President Harrison. After his public service, he rose to become President of the Pullman Palace Car Company. His only regret was that he and his mother became permanently estranged and never reconciled their differences during her lifetime.

John Nicolay had a successful career as diplomat, Marshal of the US Supreme Court, and author. He went to his grave deeply committed to preserving the legacy of Abraham Lincoln. He spent a number of months trying to find Lora Withering, the beautiful woman whom he had met on the street in Washington. She was a phantom. He never saw her again. She did not exist.

Kate Chase married Rhode Island Governor William Sprague in November of 1863. She truly was a belle about town and many high-profile gentlemen were her suitors until she settled upon Governor Sprague. Her contributions regarding women's rights are pure conjecture.

After the war, Jefferson Davis was charged with treason. He spent two years in jail, and was released before he was ever tried for that charge. After spending some time in Europe, he settled in Biloxi, Mississippi, and ultimately died in New Orleans in 1889. Interestingly, he was offered a pardon and never accepted it.

Henry Memminger and Janie Frank did not exist. But had they existed, they no doubt would have survived and thrived in post war Richmond! They had gumption.

Mary Todd Lincoln lived a sad life following the death of her husband. She suffered Tad's death in 1871, and in 1875, Robert committed her to an asylum in Illinois, hoping the institution could help her with her depression. A little over a year later, she was able to be released. She lived another six years, dying lonely and depressed in

Springfield. Mary Lincoln was 63 years old at the time of her death.

Winfield Scott died peacefully at West Point. His death came in 1866, just a year after the end of the war. There is no historical corroboration for the role I assigned to General Scott. By all accounts, he was a patriot; he was just too old to be of service by the time the Civil War was commenced.

Irvin McDowell died in San Francisco, twenty years after hostilities had ceased. He managed to bungle a second battle at Manassas in August of 1862, and then, a year before the war ended, he was transferred to the west coast, far away from day-to-day combat. Perhaps his greatest contribution was in being the landscape architect of the Presidio parkland, a greenspace that exists in San Francisco to this day.

There are suggestions that McDowell's sympathies toward the southern cause ran deep. We will never know. We do know that the result (twice!) at Bull Run was not good for the Union cause.

While very little time is spent on Ambrose Burnside in this narrative, it may interest the reader to know that he had large whiskers streaming down his face by his ears and extending to his mustache and beard. At some point following the civil war, those facial hairs would become known as sideburns. While Burnside would not be remembered for any battlefield accomplishments, his facial hair lives on forever!

Robert E. Lee was also indicted as a war criminal but never served time in jail, and charges were dropped. His family homestead was confiscated after the war. A reader today would know that land as the Arlington National Cemetery. (A little-known fact is that the property had been purchased by George Washington's stepson, and developed by his step grandson. Robert E. Lee married George Washington's step great-granddaughter and took on responsibility for the estate in 1857.) Shortly after the war, he was asked to step in as President of

Washington College in Lexington, Virginia. It was named after George Washington, and had fallen upon hard times during the war. Lee's leadership turned its fortunes around, and to this day Washington and Lee (as it became known soon after Lee helped it achieve firm financial footing) is one of the best colleges in the United States.

There is a trend in present day United States to disavow virtually anyone who is associated with our development as a nation. This narrow, misguided view is an attempt to judge the entirety of our remarkable history through the lens of the here and now. That is a myopic way to treat past events. We must always consider the actions of those we study in the context of the times in which they lived.

We presently are witnessing school boards in the United States voting to remove Abraham Lincoln's name from elementary, middle, and high schools. Why? He apparently did not move fast enough to emancipate those who were enslaved. Oh, it is easy to be a Monday morning quarterback. But it is wrong. The game was played yesterday, on yesterday's field, with yesterday's players. Abraham Lincoln was a magnificent man; a strong, visionary leader with pragmatic principals. All one needs to do is study his writings, convictions, and actions. He said what he meant, and did what he said. If only an Abraham Lincoln could emerge today to remind our citizens of the genius that helped guide us into becoming the Union we are today.

Carla Harris presently serves as a Vice Chairman of Wealth Management at Morgan Stanley, one of the largest financial service companies in the world. She talks very concisely about pertinent diversity related issues. One of her admonitions is centered on encouraging people to be more honest and candid about our challenges as a society. She says we need to "call a thing a thing." It is a wonderfully refreshing thought. You see, slavery in 1861 was a thing. We cannot pretend it wasn't. If one takes the time to read Washington and Jefferson (to name two Founding Fathers, both

Virginians) one would know that even in the 1780's, they knew slavery had to be abolished. They knew it was wrong. They meant what they said when they declared "All men are created equal." But they also knew their efforts to forge ahead with a Constitutional Republic required compromise. And in 1787, the only way to make the dream of a United States a reality was to create a more perfect Union that (for the time being, at least) included that peculiar, horrible institution. These two men, and many others, were not evil. They are historic figures who do not deserve to be relegated to the dustbin of history by latter-day revisionists who choose to castigate them for socio-economic events of their time.

It is worth a moment to discuss the concepts of compromise and conviction. Our great nation was founded by leaders, none of whom achieved what each thought to be the perfect outcome. The Declaration of Independence and Constitution are both products of negotiation and compromise. All great legislation since the Houses of Congress were formed have resulted from compromise. Yet today, extremists on the right and left have turned the word into one signaling weakness and defeat. Gone are the days when a Ronald Reagan could sit down with rough and tumble Bostonian Tip O'Neill (Democrat Majority leader of the House of Representatives during the Reagan administration) and hammer out a deal that was good for the American people. Neither side got everything it wanted, but the peoples' interests were served.

For us to progress as a nation, Republicans and Democrats alike need to restore civility and compromise as fundamental tenets for successful negotiations. Our more strident populists (on both the left and right) must stop viewing compromise and conviction as mutually exclusive. Indeed, the best of our leaders have been people of strong convictions who also understood the art of compromise is a positive characteristic. Let us hope sanity returns in Washington, D.C.

And Lastly...

Several questions remain to this day regarding the conduct of Lincoln's generals during the formative stages of the conflagration. Why did they refuse to take early, bold, decisive actions that could have crushed the rebellion before it gained traction? This story is just that; a story. But it does make one wonder what forces were at work that stymied the President's plans? Had he survived his presidency, perhaps he would have opined, and we would have learned more. It is fascinating that of all the people to run against Lincoln in his 1864 re-election campaign, it was George McClellan; Mr. do-nothing Popinjay. In a way, you can't make it up; or can you?

Made in United States
Orlando, FL
11 February 2023

29882076R00114